A Floating Phrase

A Floating Phrase

Trent Portigal

Winchester, UK
Washington, USA

First published by Roundfire Books, 2016
Roundfire Books is an imprint of John Hunt Publishing Ltd., Laurel House, Station Approach,
Alresford, Hants, SO24 9JH, UK
office1@jhpbooks.net
www.johnhuntpublishing.com
www.roundfire-books.com

For distributor details and how to order please visit the 'Ordering' section on our website.

Text copyright: Trent Portigal 2015

ISBN: 978 1 78535 422 9
Library of Congress Control Number: 2016931758

A CIP catalogue record for this book is available from the British Library.

Design: Stuart Davies

Printed and bound by CPI Group (UK) Ltd, Croydon, CR0 4YY, UK

We operate a distinctive and ethical publishing philosophy in all
areas of our business, from our global network of authors to
production and worldwide distribution.

Chapter 1

Cesarine takes a break from staring at the shadowy ceiling of her bedroom and glances at the clock radio. Fifteen minutes until the alarm is set to go off. She sighs, leans over and fumbles with the radio's on switch. Voices from the international segment of the morning current-affairs show fill the room. She finds them overly argumentative for the predawn, but, having expended the only energy she has at the moment, settles back into staring at the ceiling.

"It's going to be another Yalta. We gave all of Eastern and a large chunk of Central Europe to the Soviets last time. The only real question is: what are we going to give them this time?"

"I think that the conference could be an opportunity to discuss broader issues, to deepen the detente."

"Have you read any of their newspapers lately? The detente is just a game they play for our benefit. Their politics rest on ideology, and in their ideology we will always be the enemy. Of course, it isn't much better here: the East is still the bogeyman of choice for the vast majority of our politicians, despite their supposed diversity of opinion."

"Well, we haven't had any more crises, so I would say that it is working rather well. That doesn't mean, though, that there isn't room for improvement; improvement that won't happen if we refuse to sit at the same table and discuss issues."

The debate continues. The speech rhythms wash over Cesarine while the content sinks to the floor. It has the same level of impact as the morning reminder that shoes can be bought at the shoe store from before she emigrated. The sounds' energy slowly reinvigorates her, enough in any case for immediate reality to take hold. A mechanical reality; a series of almost but never quite identical events repeated *ad nauseam*. She is no different, needing her mainspring wound for her gears to

1

revolve. The parts are of questionable quality, so the revolutions are at best approximate. She is no longer surprised at the sporadic loss or gain of time, gear slippage and the like.

A recurring fantasy: to be able to pop off the top of her head, pull out the mechanism and futz with it. This fantasy has been prominent in her animation since the beginning. The innards have not always been gears, but also transistors, musical instruments, miniaturized large animals, rocks, etc. Sometimes one could only catch a glimpse of the inner workings through a window opened in the skull or a conveniently removable ear or eye. The fantasy took hold before the trend of disposables, when the works started to be locked in with tamper-resistant screws doubled with copious amounts of glue. A trend that passed Cesarine by, stuck as she has been in her robotic inertia.

The objects of her characters' worlds were comparable; humming with internal movement regardless of how static they might seem on the outside. Sometimes everything was compatible, or at least in rhythm. Swapping in a gear from a streetlight might very well allow our hero to come up with the idea that had up until that moment escaped her. More often than not though, there was perpetual discord, categorical differences that the hero could see through every window in the pavement and the trees – a disconcerting reminder of the superficiality of the resolution of her particular plot line.

In the old country, critics occasionally suggested that this background detracted from the principal narrative arc. Worse, it could be seen as undermining one of the fundamental tenets of the state: normal relations between everyone and everything. The mumblings and grumblings were marginal, pushed to the side by a spectacle of seeing inside things. A spectacle that ended up making her the darling of the establishment. It also didn't hurt that politics did not play a significant role in Cesarine's films or life.

Looking back, the only thing that seemed unquestionably

significant was technical curiosity. For instance, rounded river rock was ideal for coming out of a tap, or other situations where rocks needed to flow freely. At the other end of the spectrum, an aggregate with a high percentage of angular faces was great for locking up under pressure; lovely for roads. Somewhere in the middle was rock that represented thought. Rocks stable under pressure, with decent energy transfer through the system, yet sufficiently dynamic, bordering occasionally on pseudo-random, in their movements and connections. The technical side was then covered in a veneer thick enough to make the movements adequately entertaining for the audience, so they would see it as more than a technical demonstration.

"What is significant now," Cesarine declares to the shadows fading in the increasingly pronounced pre-dawn light, "is to get up and go to work."

Cesarine recalls an old article in a national newspaper from September 23, 1874 recounting a visit of Marshall M___ to R___, her current home city. It was noted that, "It is not that R___ holds any antipathy for the Marshall. However, it is a city where enthusiasm never wins out." The alignment of the streets was simply "incompatible with popular effervescence." Walking to school along the same streets a century later, Cesarine qualifies her declaration with the thought that significance is of course relative. Years ago, the notion of popular effervescence would have seemed strange, as her sense of liveliness for herself and everything around her bubbled up from an internal source, a curiosity more often than not inexplicable. She suspects that this is what led her to be curious to see the inside of things, but she can't be sure.

Although her source of interest had been changing gradually over the years, it was only with the sudden break of leaving the old country for good that she really noticed her increasing reliance on popular effervescence, that her new environment was actively undermining her sense of the importance of things, and that she lacked the inner fervor to shore up what she might recognize as potentially significant. Standing in front of the rather stately – a grey, bureaucratic sort of stately – building where she works, the already rather modest significance that motivated her to leave her bed has been lost, replaced by a functional indifference. She chooses to see this as part of the age-old tradition from the old country, even if the tradition usually manifested as functional alcoholism.

The building houses the School of Marionettes. While the name has not changed since the founding of the institution, the institution itself has been absorbed into a major university. The curriculum has evolved to a point where it would be hardly recognizable to the old masters. One can still study marionettes, as well as the inseparable folkloric repertoire, but the majority of the small student body prefers more modern forms of animation. The school supports this tendency, not only in an effort to stay relevant, but because the new techniques and technology are genuinely useful for expanding the artistic experience.

Cesarine attended a very different school, where passing down the old traditions was the most important function. It had a similar, and under the circumstances far more accurate, name: The National School of Puppetry. Her ultimate niche, stop-motion, benefited greatly from the education, even if she found little guidance for her more modern explorations. It would have been nice had the evolution of techniques for her own niche been slow enough to develop a solid tradition of its own, though perhaps two millennia of small, incremental changes was unreasonable. On the other hand, there was something attractive about a form of expression that had never been hegemonic, that existed alongside and intermingled with other techniques peacefully and productively.

Entering the building, she makes her way through cinderblock corridors directly to the room of the first of two classes she is teaching today: Introduction to Armatures. The class is more of a studio these days, an opportunity for students to build basic skeletons out of wire and wood. It is all about approaching animal movement – typically human, though insects make a consistent, non-negligible showing – with primary materials that don't require significant skill to manipulate. Movement is essential in creating a character, so it is useful to become familiar with it before putting in the time and effort into building more sophisticated armatures and encasing them in foam and fabric. The class starts with videos showing just how expressive a wire can be and how a well-placed piece of wood can add recognizable form. The first challenge is to mimic the movements on the screen, the second to deviate from them in imaginative ways.

Animated behaviorism; characters that go no deeper than their actions. It is a pleasant enough reduction; instead of digging to find the inner workings, it tries to bring them to the surface. Without a fully fleshed-out surface, a well-defined environment or a voice, the actions often slip into an abstraction barely connected to experience. Here again, there is a risk of the animation becoming a tech demo. Unlike at the beginning of Cesarine's career, however, basic stop-motion techniques have already been thoroughly explored. While she could probably coast on name recognition and impeccable – read: borderline obsessive compulsive – execution, nobody today would find it interesting. As for her students, the vast majority concentrate their efforts in other areas of animation. Still, there are usually a couple of former students a year who mention how much the basic skill of creating consistent movement in real three-dimensional space has influenced their later, largely two-dimensional, work.

Regardless of interest, Cesarine recognizes the importance of producing work from time to time if she does not want her name to be buried by the tide of other peoples' creations. The school also encourages new work rather forcefully, particularly from a foreigner with an oversized reputation and a questionable grasp of the local language. Happily, she was able to improve her language skills fairly quickly and turned out to be a competent teacher. Administration was not overjoyed that the school was going to be deprived of the significant bump in prestige they were expecting when they brought her on, but slowly came to accept her as a solid albeit unremarkable contributor to the institution. One of the tricks to maintaining functional indifference is to ensure that the level of functioning that is required stays modest.

Sometimes, when coherent thoughts take hold in the time staring at the ceiling before her alarm goes off, she wonders why the culture shock of moving to this country didn't do more than make her aware of her slide into indifference; why it didn't motivate her to change, to create. It is not as if the city's pervasive lack of enthusiasm completely overshadowed the initial sensation of newness or friction caused by misaligned norms and the energy from the community at the school. Years of playing with the idea of inner workings were not enough to elucidate the enigma of her own situation.

The class is spent wandering around the tables, giving tips here and there for emulating joints and ensuring that the armatures are stable. There is little more frustrating than an armature that won't stay in place between shots. At the end, she gives an assignment of putting together short films showing a variety of basic movements, to be presented and peer-reviewed during the next class. There is some time before her next course, Theories of Esthetics, so she makes her way through the cinderblock corridors to her still-bare, practically empty office.

Cesarine sits at the desk, pulls a well-worn book on pragmatic esthetics out of her bag, lays it on the desk and gazes at it as if it has a small window through which the words assemble and reassemble themselves with rhythmic, hypnotic movements. Hundreds of words on the page are dancing around each other, avoiding conflict with grace, pausing just long enough to take in the sense of their new order before moving on.

The reverie is interrupted by a knock at the door, followed by Anne, the department secretary, poking her head in: "Hi, Cesarine. Someone came to the main office looking for you."

Cesarine checks her watch before replying, "Who? Why didn't they just come here? Anyway, doesn't matter, I have to go to class."

"Well, his name is Valery Grandville, he's with the government and he is here, behind me."

Anne opens the door wider to show a man wrapped tightly in a heavy winter coat.

"Ah," Cesarine says matter-of-factly, "you look cold, Mr. Grandville."

Valery smiles. "It seems that you have a class to teach."

"Right. You can wait in here if you like."

"Oh, I think he will probably be more comfortable in the break room," Anne suggests, sensitive to the lifelessness of Cesarine's office. "And we can put the kettle on."

"That sounds marvelous, thank you for the offer," Valery says to Anne, then turns to Cesarine: "I'll see you in...an hour?"

Cesarine nods distractedly, wondering idly why her mind isn't giving her a show of what could be inside this government official. It seems to her that that should be more interesting than the inner life of a book she has read through countless times. As she walks to the classroom, book in hand, she ponders why her first reflection concerned the fickleness of her hallucinations rather than the implications of an apparently random visit by a bureaucrat. After her situation was normalized – an expedited process thanks to her renown in certain circles and the school's sponsorship – and once it was evident that she was going to keep a low profile, the government, along with pretty much everyone else, left her alone. It also helped that she took up residence in a provincial city short on popular effervescence, far from the avant-garde artists of the capital.

"Why do artists turn away from nature?" a student asks following a brief setting of the scene for a discussion on the weekly reading.

"Can you develop that thought some more?" Cesarine asks.

"Um, okay, well, the process of creating art is linked to the artist's experience with their surroundings, which the author basically says is nature, right? The process is just taking parts of experience accumulated over time, passions and maybe some other stuff in an esthetic way and making art out of them. But he says that art is not nature. So, I don't know, nature is incomplete? It is not enough for the artist?"

"Do you consider yourself an artist?" Cesarine considers the question of art versus nature profoundly uninteresting.

"Well, yes, or, at least, yes."

"As a thought experiment then, imagine the process of creating a work of art. Where do you get your inspiration?" Given her tendency to find everything uninteresting though, she recognizes that she is probably a lousy judge of such things.

"That's just the thing: I mainly play off what other people have created before me. That is my environment, I guess. It's not always art, not pragmatically anyway, not enough passion I imagine."

"You do not think that you get inspiration from nature, then?" It's true that nature is a useful enough context under certain circumstances.

"It's kind of unavoidable. Everything in my environment is nature, according to the author."

"Including art?" And there are specific reasons why the context is useful here, so long as one doesn't take it too far.

"I'm not sure; I don't think it's very clear."

"Compare it to the transcendental theories we were discussing last week. Do you think that this theory suggests that art is fundamentally different than nature?" Cesarine is fond of the simplistic notion that nature is the contrary of pure, man-made mechanics.

"Not really, it is more a bunch of things, including nature, mixed in a particular way. It is linked to nature, includes nature, but then, well, maybe something can include stuff yet be completely different. Maybe that's how consciousness works, you know, in relation to the brain."

"That might be going a bit far. Can we say at the very least that this theory does not treat art as an absolute ideal, or at least an object approaching such an ideal?" Any part of nature in her work is, at its heart, mechanical.

"Yeah, it's not like the transcendental theories. It is far more grounded, I'd say."

"Yet, art is not a part of nature simply cut out and put on a plate?" Which is to say that there is no nature; all trees are plastic.

"Right...it is more than that."

"So, to borrow from the reading, why don't we use the expression 'nature transformed'?" Plastic trees with inner workings just as capable as the cello in her student's head of producing the strong, accented tonic, crisply played on-beat and resonating across the softer notes that follow.

"Right! So it is nature, it is just not part of nature, in the sense of being simply a part of past experience. It is a new experience, new passion, new intention, new connections. The base material is natural and it ends up becoming one of these past experiences, but as something new in the environment."

The discussion transitions from the creation of art to its appreciation; the particularities of experiencing such an object. Cesarine is more focused on the unfortunate state of affairs where she can only infer the cello from external behavior. The performance of her student has little more depth than that of a bare armature. More, in that he is fleshed out, has clothes, and is surrounded by a well-defined scene. Less, insofar as his movements are heavily constrained, to a certain extent by these very same elements.

At least there is interaction, feedback. The ebb and flow of the discussion on the radio that morning was pleasant enough when she didn't have the energy to be an active participant, but would have been tedious had she been more awake. The streets taken on her way to work were equally agreeable as an efficient and unengaging conduit devoid of obstacles or distractions. Guiding a student with a defined, if hidden, source of autonomy to a perfectly coherent movement is an experience that brings her the closest at this point in her life to what a pragmatist would call esthetic.

It almost feels like cheating. Genuine artists work diligently to build up a character to the point where it has enough personality for actions and words to flow almost effortlessly, like the figure in the marble just waiting to be released from her cocoon. An already formed student, out of tune perhaps, a misaligned sound post here and there, offers a shortcut, even if the connection is but a lesser approximation of the intimacy shared between artist and creation. Cesarine does not believe that she has ever experienced that level of intimacy with her characters, so she would consider a lesser approximation to be more than adequate if it succeeded in breaking her out of her indifference. Instead, it only allows her to see the faint outline of a passionate sun through the clouds; making her aware of its presence even though she can barely feel its warmth.

The products of her curiosity, her drive to peer inside things and mechanize nature, have never struck her as particularly sublime. She has preferred for quite some time to view herself as a technician, rather than an artist, even if her work has always had esthetic qualities that could fall into one of the more generous definitions of art. This is of course not something that she admits to others, since her professional life is to a great extent constructed on the fact that a non-negligible portion of the population does consider her films sublime.

In the early days, she had regular moments of terror, especially when heading onstage to accept an award in front of a large crowd, that everything was in reality a setup to build her up and then expose her as a fraud in the most public and embarrassing way possible. Over time, the terror was diluted into anxiety, before settling into a very manageable awkwardness when interacting with people who are attached to an opinion far more idealistic than her own regarding her work.

The class discussion is cut abruptly at fifty minutes. Cesarine makes her way to the break room, nudging her mind in the direction of seeing something more in her mystery bureaucrat. At the entrance to the room, she is drawn to the innumerable papers dispersed on the central table in a manner that borders on – but she can't imagine actually is – chaotic; within less than an hour, he has turned the space into his office. She looks up to see him absorbed in marking up a document, perfectly comfortable in his surroundings, despite still being bundled up in his heavy coat.

She quietly sits down across from him, wanting to take a moment to observe him before engaging in any sort of conversation. The coat acts like a lead blanket, leaving only the head to be analyzed. For that, all she can imagine is solid wood, like the wood she carved in her days as a student building marionettes for traditional tragi-comic pieces. She wonders if her mind is telling her that his actions are being controlled by unknown hands, that his driving mechanism is inscrutable or simply located elsewhere, or that this is the sort of dissatisfying, unimaginative response she should expect when she tries to nudge her brain out of its torpor.

The moment of observation passed and the document reviewed, Valery settles back in his chair and looks at her with a friendly smile: "You know, I am really honored to have the opportunity to talk to such a renowned and innovative artist."

Chapter 2

The old medina is deserted as Valery and his newly obligatory bodyguard, Jack, make their way through the labyrinth of streets in the late afternoon. 'Streets' might be too generous a word, given their narrowness and the steps used to bring the pavement back in line with the slope of the hill. The narrowness is quite pleasant, since it limits the streets' exposure to the sun, keeping everything relatively cool. Valery cannot imagine the torture of trudging up the hill in his suit with the sun beating down on his head.

"We shouldn't be here," Jack mutters, eying the endless parade of blind corners and rooftop patios strung with laundry, realizing with increasing uneasiness the futility of trying to protect his client if almost anything were to happen.

"We go where the job takes us," Valery replies. "The old medina is in any case more a symbol than anything else. That is why the media focused so much attention on it during the war of independence."

"Are you saying that it was never dangerous?" Jack continues to scan the street as best he can.

"Not at all. It was simply no more dangerous for the colonizers of the time than most other area of the city outside the European town. It was more romantic to mediatize the conflict in a neighborhood that already had an exaggerated reputation, mainly from the travelogues that started to become popular in the last century, as being different and mysterious. Who wants to hear about skirmishes in the slums at the edge of town filled with recently migrated rurals? Or in housing complexes hastily and shoddily built to try to undermine support for the independence movement?"

"Huh. And after the war?"

"Oh, the neighborhood became terribly rundown for a while;

no money or skill to maintain the buildings. Then UNESCO designated it a World Heritage Site and came in to train local craftspeople the traditional techniques that had been lost. We contributed to that effort, by the way. Since then, for better or worse, it has gentrified quite a bit. There is more petty crime associated with tourism than anything else, these days."

"You've been here for a while, then?"

"I've spent most of my career in North Africa, yes. You?"

"This is the first time I have been stationed outside of Europe."

"And you were doing the same thing there?"

"Not really, it was more ceremonial. A lot of standing at entrances in uncomfortable uniforms."

"So you chose to come here?"

"Yeah. There is something to be said for being able to talk and walk around. I know that the assignment came up because of the uptick in violence and kidnappings, which are largely limited to the mountains and the desert. So really, I shouldn't be so concerned. That doesn't stop me from thinking that, from a security perspective, the medina is not an ideal place to be."

"Noted," Valery says with a smile. "In any case, we have arrived."

They are standing in front of a nondescript, two-story building that blends organically with its neighbors. The second story is cantilevered over the street, providing the small wooden door an extra layer of shadow that gives the impression that it is even smaller than it really is. Valery knocks loudly, then waits patiently for a dignified older gentleman to open the door several minutes later. Everything about the man, from his movements to the cut of his moustache, conveys an impeccable yet relaxed demeanor, in harmony with the airy inner courtyard where he leads his guests. He invites them to sit at a small café table at the edge of the courtyard, on which is spread a tea service.

Jack hesitates, unsure as to whether he should stand at a distance or sit with the others, until Valery motions for him to join them. He then follows Valery's lead in sitting quietly as their host prepares mint tea. Only once the three cups are filled does Valery start talking.

"Robert, normally I would say that, while you really should start communicating with your family back in the old country, it would be unfortunate to deprive us of the pleasure of our conversations. I can't say though that I take pleasure in being the bearer of bad news."

"Someone has died?"

"Your sister, Esther. I am sorry for your loss."

Robert's jaw clenches. He then takes a sip of his tea. By the time he places the cup on the table, the only sign of what Valery takes to be grief has disappeared.

"What do you think of the Russians' attempt to set up a new international conference on security in Europe?"

Valery is accustomed to Robert's habit of avoiding talking about his family. He has, after all, been visiting him for years, since he was first posted here as a junior diplomat immediately following the country's independence. Still, since it was almost always Esther asking the embassy to check on her brother, he felt that her passing away might shock Robert into abandoning the well-worn routine of limiting their conversations to current events, and particularly international politics. He is disappointed but not terribly surprised.

"I think that it is strange. While it is true that there are several conventions that have never been formalized between the powers, the reality on the ground follows them anyway. It seems that the Russians would have a lot to lose just for the sake of legitimizing them."

Valery, in turn, will not talk about current affairs in Africa, since his country is active in a wide variety of initiatives on the continent. It seems odd, since he represents a European country, that there wouldn't be at least as many initiatives in Europe. The situation reflects the radically different power dynamics of the two continents and the influence of small countries in general. Especially in regards to security, it has almost always been the case that large countries trump small ones in Europe. Small countries generally just follow the typically biased consensus of whatever coalition they happen to belong to, as they have neither the economic nor military clout to go their own way. In Africa, there are countless projects, such as contributing to the training of local craftspeople to reverse the deterioration of the medina, that are both within reach for a country with limited means and result in real, if minor, improvements.

The conversation continues until the next call to prayer. Robert then sees them to the door as he has always done. Valery repeats that he is sorry for the loss of Esther. Robert nods almost imperceptibly before closing the door. The two men make their way down the hill in the fading light of the day, neither feeling the need to converse. Jack is even less at ease, but has come to terms with the reasons for the visit.

The next morning, Valery is settling into his office when Rose, a junior who has been at the embassy for the past five years, knocks on the open door and enters without waiting for a response. She puts a cable on his desk in front of him, then leaves. It isn't Rose's responsibility to deliver cables and, since they are coded, cannot read them herself. She just hopes that the next one will give instructions that she is to be reassigned to someplace more interesting, and so the faster they are brought to Valery's attention, the sooner she can pack her bags.

Valery understands the attitude, and imagines that he himself was once like that, in some dimly remembered previous life. Everyone has to go through the consular-services phase; processing visa- and passport-renewal applications for the most part; and most hope for something more. Rose was assigned here as a Russia specialist when the competition for influence between the major powers was heating up. What she found, when she was able to get through her allotment of paperwork and look out into the world, was, as she put it, inane dick measuring. It was mainly a competition between big infra-structure projects in the middle of nowhere, connecting nothing and serving no one. If, by miracle, a project could actually be used, the users found out soon enough that it was stuffed full of proprietary technology that served the local industry of whichever country magnanimously donated the structure and that no one could afford to repair it. She would prefer being part of a mission where there was a modicum of diplomatic subtlety.

Valery methodically decodes and then reads the cable. He reads it again, slower, making sure that he is capturing every-thing. After the second time through, he lays the paper on his cluttered desk and chuckles. Rose is going to get her wish, assuming that continuing to work for him does not invalidate it in some way. He does not want to exclude the possibility that he is somehow part of the problem. Knowing that she has not gone far, he walks to the door, catches her already watching eye and motions for her to join him. Once she is in the office, he closes the door.

"It has been a long time since I was surprised by the content of a cable. They are usually so predictable that I wonder if it is really worth the time and effort to code them. Anyway, it looks like we are being reassigned, to Europe of all places. The prelim-inary discussions between the major powers concerning the conference everybody has been talking about have resulted in an agreement that every country – large and small, partisan and neutral – is to be involved equally. A complete break from Munich, Yalta... It's not explicit, but, by the tone of the cable, the minister was caught completely off-guard and is scrambling to put together a respectable delegation. And that includes us."

Valery pauses to let the news sink in. Rose holds in her excitement and questions, only betraying her eagerness by leaning further forward in her chair.

"Apparently, the conference is going to be split into three areas: security, economy and, well, human rights."

Rose leans back with a sigh. "We're going to be responsible for the third, aren't we?"

"Yes."

"I knew that it was too good to be true. I mean, don't get me wrong: I'm still happy to go. But to be stuck with the touchy-feely part that will never be implemented and cannot be enforced..."

"Maybe the ministry has some practical ideas; it's not as if the cable goes into details. The very fact that the all the powers have agreed to put it on the agenda is interesting."

"Eh. It is an easy thing to give in return for the chance of formal recognition for everything else."

"Perhaps, but there are reasons to be cautiously optimistic and, if it does lead somewhere, that would change the way the game is played. Yesterday, I would have said that there was no chance that small and neutral countries would have a real say in continental politics. Today, I am not so sure. Maybe we shouldn't assume that the old Westphalian rules of non-interference in the internal affairs of states will hold. I would hate to be wrong twice; I don't think that my reputation could take it."

"Fine, I will try to be optimistic. So long as we don't slip into full-on naïveté. It is hard to tell where the first ends and the second begins."

"In any case, we have a more pressing question. The ministry wants a full team together for the debriefing in the capital. Only, they have a funny notion of team. They want us to include a high-profile defector who can give us insight into the intentions of the other side."

"I'm fairly sure that no high-profile defector in their right mind would come to our country."

"It is a quandary."

"This is because the major powers are including defectors in their delegations and our politicians don't want to be left out, isn't it?"

"I imagine so."

"Remind me again why I should be optimistic."

"I just can't think of anyone at the moment. Maybe an idea will come."

"Who else do we need to include?"

"Someone more familiar with Germany and currently on mission in Europe. I was thinking Etienne."

"He's with NATO, right? I've heard good things. Does the defector need to be a dissident?"

"I suppose that that would help, less chance that they are working both sides. Probably can't just be a dissident though. Someone like Solzhenitsyn or Amalrik."

A moment passes in silence as both try to think of someone who would fit the profile. They work on the unspoken assumption that, if they have to look through the records, the person would not really be prominent.

"Well," Rose finally says with some hesitation. "A couple of years ago, I went to an animation retrospective in the capital. I recall vaguely that one of the animators was originally from a small Eastern country but was at the time teaching at a university in the north. Everyone seemed to think that her work was really important. I thought her films were just odd, but not necessarily in a bad way. I don't know if she was ever a dissident or anything like that. And I, wait, it's on the tip of my tongue; Cesarine. Cesarine Vaculka."

"I have never heard of her."

Chapter 3

"Plenary session is a bit of a misnomer," Cesarine remarks to herself as she makes her way through another file from the innumerable boxes surrounding her. She half listens to the session piped through the conference-center CCTV to a small black and white screen and an even smaller speaker. It was only after a microphone feedback screech during setup that she discovered the TV, tucked in a corner, hidden behind the boxes. She arranged the boxes in neat rows on the other side of the room and dragged her table to the screen so she was not completely cut off from the outside world.

She was charged with finding anything that might be of any use in the negotiations. Since her country's delegation has yet to decide on the appropriate title for the third area – let alone anything more substantial – she has no idea what might be useful. According to Valery, these things are usually decided at the last minute, which is to say after the ceremonial opening session. Of course, since the real reason for her being stuck in this room is the inability of the head of the delegation and the minister to decide on whether her presence at the session would be seen as a provocation, it would not surprise her if the choice of title takes an eternity. In lieu of coming to a conclusion on reasonable grounds as to where she should be, they convinced themselves that important background research needed to be done and that she was the perfect candidate for the task.

She should not feel unique as a potential provocateur, since the disagreement regarding the title has more or less the same source. The more aggressive countries want 'Freer movement of people, ideas and information'. The more passive countries feel that 'free movement' is an unnecessary provocation with cold war undertones and prefer 'human and cultural development'.

The neat rows she created are filled with internal chaos, so she actually has motivation to go through the boxes and put together instruments for her orchestra of noise. It is an unusual sensation, since the content of an object or person has rarely been very important in determining what she imagines it to be. The uniformity of the boxes, full of monotonous reports and files, gives her imagination little to work with. The content that she has gone through thus far, in contrast, has subtle nuances that, under the circumstances, blare at her, drowning out the frail, tinny voices from the television.

Over time, the blaring coalesces into a cacophony of voices without solid mechanics behind them. Each carton becomes a black box of conversations, arguments, speeches and monologues. Regardless of their clarity, though, none of them are comprehensible without being paired with the words on the page. She begins to sort the files and reports based on loudness, with the most intense voices being placed in the row the furthest from the television. She labels that row conflicts and collabora-tions. The next row is events and ceremonies, followed by unexpected absences and, finally, predictable isolation.

With the cacophony increasingly concentrated on the other side of the room, the sounds from the television become better defined. Whenever the individual she takes to be the host of the conference speaks, she is distracted from the document in front of her. He is, as she has pieced together from biographical tidbits scattered throughout a variety of collaborations and ceremonies, the former head of state of a very small country with sizable linguistic groups. She is vaguely aware that it is his ability to switch between languages with incompatible rhythms while somehow keeping an even flow that attracts her. The more focused she is on the voice, the more its transformation by the speaker into a thin, reedy sound somewhere in the upper register of the tenor range grates.

She turns off the television, unplugs it and looks to see if something can be done. Seeing that the speaker is tacked on to the tube with regular screws, she searches her bag for one of the multi-tools she generally keeps scattered around. She unscrews the speaker, cuts the wires soldered to it, strips them and then, somewhat belatedly, reflects on what to attach the wires to. Concluding that, as this is a conference center, there must be an audio/visual equipment room somewhere, she leaves the half-reorganized papers and ventures out into the world.

The center is built on the upper slope of a hill heading down to a lake, with the main hall completely open to take advantage of the view of the city fanned out on the lower slope and the water beyond. The less public an operation is, the further it is burrowed in the hill. Cesarine's room is located at the midpoint of this arrangement. She takes a moment to look at the water, rather idyllic with waves sufficiently pronounced to give a sense of movement but not so much as to lead to violence. She wonders if the Marshall would have found her city more inspiring if, instead of being flat, it was built on a hillside, with the roads leading to this expanse in perpetual movement.

The thought passes and she looks inward. The hall is filled for the most part with center staff taking advantage of the session to move about freely. Some are placing refreshments on a long table in the center of the space, others are just using the hall as a shortcut, since it is a more direct route than the service hallways to a variety of areas. Occasionally, a junior leaves the session and makes a beeline for their delegation's backroom to search for a detail missing from the briefing sheets. A number of journalists are sitting in isolation along the walls, finishing up dispatches in relative peace and while the pertinent quotations are still fresh, before heading to the chaos of the media room to send them off. They all seem to be in their own bubble of concentration, racing to meet the inevitably short deadline of whatever outlet they are working for. Cesarine's imagination sees them as part of the same chorus, one mechanism working in the background of the conference, setting a tone of feverish seriousness.

She approaches one of the staff at the long table to inquire about the location of the A/V room. He hesitates, unsure whether it is appropriate for a delegate to go so far into the hillside, then decides to give her directions. He figures that she is asking because some piece of equipment is not working correctly and he does not want to get involved. Even if he did, putting the food out before the break is his most pressing concern.

The rows of gear in the A/V room would have filled the Ceserine of the National School of Puppetry with indescribable joy. While the professors tolerated – even encouraged from time to time – her interest in stop-motion animation, the school held to the philosophy that a surfeit of technology was detrimental to storytelling. The challenge of getting together adequately functioning equipment for a projection of her work often approached that of its creation. It wasn't until she found a wider audience, well after her student days, that she could just hand a reel to a projectionist and worry more about the reception of the film than whether it would be torn apart by the machine two minutes in.

"Do you have a powered speaker that we can use in my delegation's backroom?" Cesarine asks the attendant behind the desk at the front of the room. That feverishness died down years ago, making mimicking the seriousness of the chorus simple.

"Yes," the attendant answers without question and immediately heads to a row of small speakers. He brings one back and sets it on the table for Cesarine to inspect.

Cesarine confirms that it has connectors for bare wires. "This will do."

The attendant writes the code in the log while asking Cesarine if she needs any cables. She shakes her head, writes her particulars in the log and leaves with the speaker.

As she makes her way out of the hill, her progress is slowed by people milling in the hall. The variety of expressions and gestures indicates that they are the main players in the drama;

delegates taking a break from the session. There are undoubtedly too many of them in a space lacking a central focus for a unified narrative. Instead, they indulge in secondary plots that add a certain depth to the characters that is lacking in high-level discussions on concepts such as 'free movement'. It is difficult to take in the complexity of the scene from within the crowd, so she finds stairs to the next level to get a better look at the groupings and interactions of the mass.

At the top of the stairs, Cesarine finds herself once more among the chorus, though here, without a central table to pile with food and drink, journalists make up the majority. She walks to the railing overlooking the main hall and loses herself in the movement below, which seems to flow like a river through the window into the lake. The river is turbulent, with the stream whirling around unmovable figures and occasionally trying to escape its narrow bed.

"You are the Sorceress." An amused voice comes from behind her, cutting through the seriousness the chorus emits.

Cesarine continues to immerse herself in the regular movement of people and water in front of her, noting that the food has been barely touched.

A man Cesarine takes to be a journalist, despite his evident insouciance regarding stories and deadlines, joins her at the railing.

"Do you see phalanxes?" he asks, nodding towards a tight formation of assistants and security personnel around an apparently important man. Scanning the hall, one other formation of equal size can be seen on the other side of the table. Several smaller ones, some of whom formed around women, are scattered through the hall.

Cesarine shakes her head almost imperceptibly, preferring to envision boats. She still has to revise her original understanding of the scene to take into account the fact that many of the central figures are not as unmoving as she initially imagined. The ones on the larger boats are completely isolated from the rhythm of the water around them, while the smaller ones are only somewhat buffered from what surrounds them. It would be fascinating if a couple of them slipped into the lake and slowly made their way to the other side, to be lost to her view.

"I hope that the two big ones meet. The discussion over how to get around each other would probably reach a level of diplomacy far superior to the interminable posturing of the session. Or they'd put on a nice display of Roman-style tactics. The latter would probably be more entertaining, I have to admit."

Cesarine does not respond, lacking the motivation to view the crowd differently. They both look down into the discrete worlds their imaginations have created. The journalist quietly tries to coax one of the large groups to move to the other side of the table as if it was a recalcitrant dog. Cesarine, far less invested in her world, wonders idly if this stranger really is a journalist and if, as a delegate, she should be acting in any particular way. She concludes that it is best to stay silent until she is clearer on how to function in her new role. It is clear to her that he is equally lost; aping the journalistic habit of sitting off to the side as the all too quick cut-off approaches to finalize a piece, yet missing the emotional content that would place him as part of the chorus, not to mention the dedication to his craft that would have prevented him from noticing her.

"Well, our antagonists are far too stubborn to take my subtle hints," the not-quite-journalist sighs melodramatically. "Or maybe they are just tired; after all, it takes a lot of energy to grandstand over nothing for hours on end. They are not even touching the food. It's actually kind of sad."

"Don't you have an article to write?" Cesarine finally asks, her curiosity getting the better of her.

"Ha! You can understand me. And yes, I do, I should really get back to it. But, meeting you, here, the Sorceress, in the flesh! There will be other articles, other deadlines; the outlet can pull this one from the wire. They would probably do that anyway, something about my work undermining the dignity of a serious journal. Shocking, I know."

"Oh. Well, I have to get back," she replies, vaguely uncomfortable with the oversharing.

As she walks away, she hears him call after her, "So, you are the Sorceress, right?"

She focuses her attention on the power cord of the speaker, which has chosen this moment to unwind, while braving the current of delegates in her feeble one-person craft.

Chapter 4

"What the hell?" Rose asks angrily as Cesarine enters the delegation's backroom. Cesarine continues to the television, puts down the speaker and then joins Rose by the partially reorganized files.

"What the hell?" Rose repeats, gesturing emphatically.

"I noticed that they were badly organized when I started to go through them, so I have been sorting them."

"Okay," Rose says with a bitter edge, "I need all the material we have on Poland. Please bring the relevant files over to the table. I would do it myself, but it appears that we no longer have Poland-specific boxes."

"Just Poland?" Cesarine asks, recognizing that her system does not work well for Rose's request.

"Just Poland."

"I mean, not Poland as part of a series of multi-party or bilateral events, or even in isolation?"

"Look, there is a reason everything was arranged by country, and then by bloc: they are the actors in our little game."

Valery and Etienne walk in at that moment.

"Okay, something's up with Poland," Valery declares to the room. "And what happened to the TV?"

"Yes, something's up with Poland," Rose replies.

"They have historically had closer relations with the West," Etienne points out.

"Because of their Catholicism?" Rose asks.

"Partly. I recall that the chair of the Party had a link with France, maybe studied there or had some relatives or ancestors from there..."

"Check the files," Valery says.

"The files are not well-organized," Rose replies. "I imagine that the ministry just dumped everything they thought might be remotely useful in boxes, added some random odds and ends for color, and then sent them along, assuming that by the time the boxes got here, the contents would be sufficiently shaken together. Which is to say that it will take us a bit of time to find the pertinent documents."

With Etienne's recollections, Cesarine has a good idea where the files are – assuming that they are among the documents she has already sorted. They would be on the quieter side of collaborations and events, since the encounters would be bilateral and generally friendly, while lacking the occasional boisterous informality that characterizes meetings of states from the same side of the wall. She stays quiet though, so as to not undermine what she sees as Rose's misguided effort to cover for her.

Instead, she attaches the wires sticking out of the television to the new speaker and plugs it in. The conversation falls off while the three diplomats watch Cesarine, perplexed. When nothing happens after everything is connected – the sound in the meeting room is muted during the breaks – the puzzlement turns to vague disappointment. By this time, Cesarine is looking back at them and the disappointment makes way for the discomfort of being under the gaze of someone clearly analyzing them. The moment passes quickly and the conversation resumes as if nothing happened.

"In any case," Valery says, "we knew from the beginning that the East – excepting Romania of course; they made their independence clear during the pre-negotiations – was going to negotiate as a block. It is becoming increasingly clear that, while that is certainly the case, the Soviets are not able to hold the line they initially established while keeping the group together."

"So, we aren't wasting our time?" Rose asks.

"If we can bridge what we are trying to accomplish with the objectives that Poland, among others, are pushing for in the Eastern Bloc, I don't see why we would be. I suppose that it is a question of finding a balance between what works for them, which is surprisingly compatible with what we are going for, and Soviet tanks in the streets of their capital."

"Isn't that sort of insight what Cesarine is here for?" Etienne asks.

The three turn once more towards Cesarine with a renewed expectation that something should happen. Cesarine is starting to think that the breaks in the session are far too generous and would like everyone to just leave her alone. Then she can concentrate on the thankless task of putting the documents back in the nonsensical order in which she found them and suffer the jumbled voices no matter where she is in the room. She hopes that the new speaker's rendition of the conference host's intonations counterbalances the chaos, but does not think that she will be that lucky.

"Perhaps you should have sought out a defector from a country that managed to strike that balance. You do know that my country was invaded sometime between Hungary and Czechoslovakia, right? I was holed up at the time, working on a short. *The Apartment*. I know that because the question of where I was at that time is quite popular at festivals. I usually give the title of whatever film I want to promote, but it really was *The Apartment*."

Cesarine is tempted to go into the details of the animation, some interesting anecdotes about its production, that sort of thing. She is aware, however, that she has perhaps said the worst thing possible; essentially admitting that she is useless in the role. It doesn't bother her for the most part, though with this, the reorganization of the boxes and the speaker replacement, she is forced to wonder whether she is losing the functional part of her functional indifference.

"Right," Valery says slowly. "Perhaps your contribution can be more around where we shouldn't go, what propositions will definitely not work. As far as you are able, of course. We realize that you were never particularly involved in politics. Hopefully, we can have a much broader influence than just politics at the end of the day."

A jarring cacophony suddenly comes from the new speaker, startling the three officials. Cesarine, who has been waiting for the sound to be taken off mute and the session to resume, calmly leans over to turn down the volume. She is pleased with the full sound; her misgivings make way for the curiosity as to how the conference host's voice will come across. It is clear that now is not the moment to get into her capacity to contribute to the team.

Etienne is the first of the others to react: "Looks like the session is starting back up. We should head back to the room."

Maybe it is his former posting with NATO that leads Cesarine to imagine sometimes a military headquarters, sometimes a tank crew in his head. In either case, there is a severe dressing down going on behind closed doors for having lost track of time and being overtaken and surprised by what is going on in the field.

"Right," Valery replies. "Rose, can you get something together for Poland? And Hungary, if there is time? We need to be as prepared as possible for the negotiations on the third area."

"Sure."

With that, Valery follows Etienne out of the room.

"I guess that it is just the two of us," Rose says, turning towards Cesarine. "Let's get this done, shall we?"

Before Rose can come up with a plan of attack, Cesarine goes to where she thinks the pertinent files can be found. They are indeed there, so she pulls them and brings them to the table. Rose starts looking through them.

"This is everything?" Rose asks.

"Everything linked to what Etienne suggested that I have found thus far."

"Why didn't you get them earlier?"

"I haven't finished sorting the boxes. They are, as you said, a mess."

"They really aren't. I made sure of that before they left the ministry so we wouldn't have this sort of problem. Just like I made sure that we would have the documents here, so we wouldn't have to keep running between the center and the embassy like the groups in charge of the other two areas."

"I suppose that organizing is somewhat subjective."

"This isn't art, it isn't open to interpretation. There is a standard that everyone follows. You were sort of thrown into this, so I don't blame you for not being familiar with how every-thing works. I just hope that you recognize that it doesn't help if only you can find documents. You weren't brought on to be a clerk."

Cesarine wants to ask why exactly she was brought on. Nobody has been clear on that point since Valery came to the school. The situation has only become even murkier after her arrival at the conference. A clear response would certainly help her be more functional in the environment. On the other hand, all she really needs to do is to not follow her impulses to change things around her. Instead of seeking answers, she loses herself in the hypnotisingly methodical production line she sees in Rose's head; an almost completely automated system that efficiently creates monotonous yet apparently useful objects. The objects are not used, however, but rather disassembled equally efficiently and recycled through the machines to become the same objects once more.

"What I don't understand," Rose continues, while leafing through the pages of a file and jotting down notes for a targeted briefing, "is why you aren't more interested in creating a better Europe for everyone. I would be the first to admit that there is a good chance that this conference won't amount to much and that, even if an agreement is reached that moves things in the right direction, it wouldn't change people's daily lives in a significant manner. But this is an unprecedented opportunity; this is the first time that the treatment by governments of their own citizens is on the agenda, and that so many parties are involved.

"You were lucky to be in a position to defect, having been allowed to attend a festival your work was being shown at in the West. What about everyone who will never have that chance? The situation must have been far from ideal to push you to leave family, friends, everything you had built, behind."

Cesarine shrugs, torn between a conversation she does not want to be part of and boxes she does not want to reorganize. The dilemma is resolved when the fully fleshed out voice of conference host comes through the speaker. Among the boxes, the voice would be lost.

"I did choose to come," Cesarine replies, avoiding the real question.

"Sure, that is a good first step. The next step is to advise us: what should we be aiming for to support the population of your country? What are the pitfalls that we can avoid? As an artist, you can help us choose the best locations to build bridges between artistic communities. Why could your films be seen internationally while other work was censored, even locally? The third step is to keep your expectations modest while not falling into cynicism. What you said earlier to Valery was pretty cynical. I completely understand that that cynicism is justified, given all that has happened. However, in order to make things better, you have to find a way beyond it. You have to focus on the opportunities, no matter how insignificant they might seem."

The conference host has ceded the floor to representatives of the delegations. The grandstanding the not-quite-journalist derided has begun anew, leaving Cesarine nothing to distract her from the objects cycling through Rose's head and the only slightly more original words she is expressing. Rose's approach is reasonable enough; she is evidently looking for anything that could be considered a win in the end, something to point to if the final agreement formally legitimizes the annexation of the Baltic States during the war, the border between the Germanys and everything else the Soviets are looking to get out of the exercise.

It is an approach only a notch or two above cynicism.

"And don't think that it is just you who is tempted by cynicism," Rose adds.

Cesarine can't see the downside of accepting the steps laid out, at least for the time being. All she needs to do is avoid admitting how useless she is and doing things completely incongruous with how one is supposed to act as a delegate, and perhaps put in a modicum of effort into coming up with an insight or two, regardless of how unoriginal they might be.

Rose is distracted enough with the briefing to give Cesarine time to reflect on potential sources for these insights. She could recycle portraits of life in small Eastern countries from books available locally. Fiction would probably be best, since it would be more personal. There is little chance that a book store will have writers from her own country, but they may have authors like Kundera. The situation in Czechoslovakia wasn't all that different than her own country and things haven't changed that much since he left. She might also be able to pick up some tips on how to act like someone who has defected, since he wrote on that too. It is evident that pretending to be an artist is no longer enough.

Chapter 5

"So, what's up with Poland?" Cesarine asks as she passes by the not-quite-journalist, who is again sitting against the wall, working on an article and doing his best to blend in to the chorus.

"You were seeing boats, weren't you? It has to be the lake that the crowd just sort of blended into. Which got me wondering: was the Czechoslovakia boat tandem? Is there such thing as a tandem boat? That probably doesn't make any sense, since the Slovaks kind of took over in Prague after '68. But, who cares? If a tandem boat doesn't exist, we should invent it."

"Wouldn't a canoe be considered tandem?"

"Right, a canoe! But then I imagine Canadian trappers singing 'Allouette' and collecting pelts. What were you saying about Poland?"

"Nothing."

"Good, because that is about as much as I know about the country."

Cesarine continues on her way to find a bookstore in the hope of shoring up her usefulness without expending a great deal of effort. She imagines that other people's preconceived notions of her will do half the work, as has been the case for years with her identity as an artist. Failing that, going back to her placid existence in the city without enthusiasm is an increasingly tempting alternative.

After riding a series of escalators down the hill and passing through the main entrance, she finds herself on the street in the center of this new city. It feels strange to be outside, surrounded by people who likely know little to nothing about a conference going on across the street that could either fundamentally change the politics of the continent or render permanent what was supposed to be a temporary kludge, affecting the lives of millions. She asks herself if knowing would make any difference for them; if they would care more than she does. She also wonders whether the internal mechanism of the center ends at the door or has tentacles spread across the urban landscape. Perhaps there is a hydraulic system stretching under the lake, keeping the center upright but not static.

She looks back to see if there is a slight sway in the structure, in delayed time with the waves of the lake, and is surprised to find the not-quite-journalist standing beside her.

"I can't even imagine..." he says, turning to follow where she is looking.

"Don't you have an article to write?"

"Just sent it in. I expect it to be rejected any moment now."

"You have a lot of confidence in yourself."

"I do, yes."

"So you decided to follow me?"

"It seemed the thing to do, assuming of course that you are indeed the Sorceress. I don't recall that point being settled, however."

"I can just tell you that I am not who you think I am, and then you can go off and do whatever you would otherwise be doing."

"Well, since I am here, it would be a shame for you to waste an opportunity to talk to someone who is familiar with the city."

"A shame for me?"

"You might have noticed that practically everyone here is a foreigner. And, I suspect that you have more planned than to stand outside the entrance of the center, imagining...what are you imagining, by the way?"

"I did have the intention of going to a bookstore, if you felt like pointing me in the right direction."

"I think that I should come with you. Then you will have the chance to explain to me why you are not the person I take you to be."

The not-quite-journalist starts walking down the grand

avenue that leads straight out from the center to the lake. Cesarine takes a last look at the center, which just looks heavy and imposing; lacking the fluidity to react to the energy from the lake. Then she follows him down the crowded street, caught up in the movement.

Without looking at her, he says, "I suppose that I should also give you the courtesy of introducing myself. My name is Lucien, sometimes journalist."

"And other times?"

"I have been known to pen an occasional poem here, a story there..."

"You don't seem very passionate about your articles."

"True. Then again, I live here. When a conference comes to town, I'll write about it. It is not really any different than any traveling show. For other reporters – at least the ones who followed the conference here – this sort of diplomatic back and forth is their bread and butter."

"A jack of all trades, then."

"That's about right. Unlike you, I suspect. I remember the first time I saw one of your films, and I still have trouble finding the words to describe it. I was genuinely scared; it was the first time an assignment escaped me; the imagination was simple beyond words. I didn't realize it at first; I thought that I had hit a block, that I could no longer express myself. I had such trepidation with the next job, but, needing to eat, I took it anyway. And the words flowed like they always had.

"So, being curious, I looked into who created the piece. I didn't get very far at first, and then I ran into a journalist from your country, in town to cover a conference. It was strange because until now only the big countries came to these things and, from the East, well, you know how that works. So-called journalists from the state outlets write a story that gets disseminated verbatim through the Pact countries. Anyway, yes, a journalist who was quite talkative when he had enough booze in him.

"After he had heard my story, he laughed and then went on about a famous artist who ensorcelled her audience with her films. He said that everyone called her the Sorceress. The word could also be translated as witch, I suppose, but I prefer sorceress."

"Do you know much about the history of cinema?"

"Just a little."

"George Méliès? The brothers Lumière?"

"Vaguely."

"Your sorceress is Méliès; the magician, the entertainer. I am – or was – a Lumière brother; an engineer, a technician. The two are confused far too often for my taste."

"The old adage that advanced technology is indistinguishable from magic. It seems reasonable enough that people are confused."

"This is the first time I have heard of that adage."

"It's not really that old. Still, don't you find being seen as Méliès flattering? Isn't it indicative of how far you have gone with the technical side?"

"Flattered? No. People will see what they want to see, though."

"That doesn't seem entirely true. They obviously bring something to the table; they can certainly be influenced beforehand, that sort of thing. Still, to say that what you have created is somehow unrelated..."

"It is possible that I have encouraged that tendency on occasion. How can I not, when my success rests at least in part on the misunderstanding?"

"You are living a lie. You've sold out. Capitalism trumps art."

"The title of your next article, no doubt."

"I do like my hypocrisy layered, with overtones of failed subtlety."

"Now you're just trying to be poetic."

"Pathetic, isn't it?"

"It is a step up from trying to fit in to the chorus of foreign correspondents at the center."

Lucien suddenly stops, turns to Cesarine, and asks, "What are you imagining now?"

"Is the bookstore far?" Cesarine is in fact imagining nothing. While she finds the banter mildly amusing, her disinterest in theory and the lack of culmination of ideas into a dominant note, comparable with that achieved by her students, leaves her imagination dormant.

He points to a storefront halfway down the block.

"Good." Cesarine keeps walking.

"I find it hard to believe that someone with such a vibrant imagination can believe that their work is primarily technical, with just a superficial veneer of art."

It is clear to Cesarine that Lucien believes her mind to be whirring at that very moment with an endless supply of energy and originality, producing a wealth of ideas that, when distilled into an animation, overwhelms the audience, leaving them in a state of ineffable awe. Perhaps he has to believe it, if only to justify his failure to put his experience with her work into words.

She no longer finds the conversation worth continuing, doubly so if he is indeed trying to justify, or even just plumb what he considers to be the ultimate source, of a case of writer's block. The close proximity of the bookstore draws her mind away from her assumed identity of artist and towards that of defector. She wonders what the conversation would have been like with the latter as the focus. It would not have been magic but perhaps nested dolls of foreignness – both assumed and real – that would have stolen his words. Each doll would be from a different set; none of them fitting well together, and, assembled as best as possible, still falling short of a complete identity. Although she is not sure that a fractured, incomplete identity would be that difficult for Lucien to put on paper.

The two go in different directions once they are inside the store. Cesarine heads directly to foreign literature while Lucien meanders towards philosophy. She quickly finds what she is looking for; fictional accounts of dissidence and exile that stay close enough to lived experience to freely play with the broader themes, more often than not ironically or satirically, while staying grounded. With this mix of reality and literary interpretation in hand, creating the personal history that the delegation expects, a history that avoids the pitfalls of bare facts and methodical analysis typical to non-fiction sources. She still has to play the role of artist, after all.

After paying for her books, Cesarine resists the urge to leave immediately. She catches glimpses of Lucien between the rows of books; he appears far more at home here than at the center. After a moment, he notices that she is waiting for him. He smiles, motions that he will only be a minute longer. He goes back to the philosophy section, picks up a thin book and comes to the front to pay for it. He writes a short dedication on the inside flap and then hands it to Cesarine.

"For putting up with my incessant curiosity," he explains.

Cesarine takes the book and looks at the cover: Emerson's *Nature*. She suppresses her derisive laugh and her regret for not having left earlier. She opens the cover to read the dedication:

The world around you is imbued with your magic, despite the modesty of your intentions. You will always be my Sorceress.
Lucien Thistle

She thanks him for the book with her usual lack of enthusiasm, which he does not seem to notice.

She feels a momentary irritation at the underlying assumption that magic has more value than technique, but then her whole time with Lucien has been marked by a series of annoyances. In general, she finds this sort of friction useful, if insufficient, to provoke action. She is well aware that that is one of the reasons she agreed so readily to Valery's proposal, despite her belief that her participation in the conference would end up doing nothing for her. To be offered a transcendentalist essay on nature just underlines how little the situation here differs from her life in the city without exuberance, teaching esthetic theories to future animators. It is not a bad result, though; certainly not negative enough to maintain her irritation, let alone lead her to express it. The result actually gives her more confidence that she can play the expected role, just like at the university.

Cesarine and Lucien exit the bookstore and pause on the sidewalk.

"Pass me back the book," Lucien asks. "I want to read you a short passage, two sentences, that I am rather fond of."

Cesarine gives the book to Lucien, who flips to a page close to the beginning.

"Crossing a bare common, in snow puddles, at twilight, under a clouded sky, without having in my thoughts any occurrence of special good fortune, I have enjoyed a perfect exhilaration. I am glad to the brink of fear."

He returns the book, leaving the second sentence floating in the air.

"It has been a pleasure to get to know you," Lucien continues after the pause. "Alas, I have another engagement, though I suspect that we will see each other before too long at the center. Given the speed at which diplomacy moves, I might even have the time to convince you that my dedication is true."

Cesarine walks back to the center, the phrase lost and the book dropped in her bag among those she bought to fend for itself. She listens to her purchases mocking Emerson's idealism using a similar tone to that used with characters convinced that the end of history necessarily passed through the surreal world of normalized socialism. Cesarine realizes that it would have been easy to refuse the book. She is after all a delegate and he a journalist, even if neither is particularly committed to their role. At the same time, if the conference does end up lasting months or years, it is just as well to be on reasonably good terms with someone beyond the delegation.

She turns onto the grand avenue leading back to the center. The wind has picked up, animating the flags in front of the building and making the trees on the hill on both sides sway. This moving frame gives the glass that dominates the facade an ethereal quality. She imagines that such an insubstantial barrier will give way at any moment, letting loose a torrent of people. Some will cling tighter together, resisting the breakup of their craft as it is swept over the edge into the street and protecting their senior officers. Others will grab onto the central table, the most seaworthy flotsam in reach; cursing the falling platters of food.

The avenue takes on more interest. She evaluates her options of objects to hold onto. Signs and street furniture seem too flimsy. The trees are a mix of old and new planes; the former too big to get her arms around, the latter still barely bigger than saplings. The buildings are all smooth, lacking the details that could contribute to public effervescence or give her a handhold. The doors will have already been locked by fearful shopkeepers. Clearly the best choice is to stay at the edge and let the current take her. Then she can avoid the larger vessels and aim for a side street.

Chapter 6

"We sit along the wall," Etienne says, as he and Cesarine enter a conference room dominated by a large circular table in the center. He motions to chairs behind the place at the table with an inverted cardboard 'v' printed on both sides with their country's flag and Valery's name.

Cesarine follows him and sits down. The sessions are now broken down into the three areas, so it fell to Valery to include her in the room. He thought that closer proximity to the action might trigger ideas that could contribute to the team. It is a relief for Cesarine since, after the boxes were reorganized in a way that pleased Rose, she has preferred to spend the least amount of time possible in the backroom.

"Is Rose coming?" Cesarine asks Etienne as the support staff finish up any last-minute preparation left to do and the delegates at the table chat among themselves about anything but the task at hand.

"No. She is at the embassy, compiling new information with people from the other two areas."

"She has not avoided the obligation to go back and forth between here and the embassy after all, then."

"She has at least cut down on the trips. The difference in opinion as to where to keep the background documents and coordinate our approach is understandable; while it is more convenient to do everything at the center, the embassy is more secure. Nothing is set in stone though, and these sorts of decisions have a tendency to flip back and forth depending on short-term priorities."

"No ideal solution?"

"Perhaps there is. I wouldn't want to assume. In my experience, people who search for genuinely ideal solutions end up with little to show for their time and effort. It is the nature of a job that relies on at least minimal agreement among actors with different ideals and ideologies."

Valery and the other delegates at the table have taken their places and the rotating chair calls the session to order. In the previous sessions, while Cesarine was still in the midst of the tumult of the boxes, the group had come to a high-level agreement on the right to disseminate information – effectively freedom of expression. The order of the day is to discuss limitations or responsibilities associated with that right.

The chair suggests that the table start by listing each country's existing laws on the subject, and then they can work towards common language that captures the clauses. This sparks a heated discussion as to whether limitations need to be formally enshrined in law. Cesarine is confused as to why this point is important, since legal legitimacy in one area or another is the ultimate goal for everyone involved. The delegates finally agree to the inclusion of the requirement of laws at the country level reflecting limitations, so long as the expressions used for the limitations, such as 'national security' and 'public order', are left undefined in the document.

Cesarine glances at Etienne, who seems to be completely absorbed by the discussion and is taking methodic notes. Focusing on the notes, she feels incredibly foolish with her lackluster attempt to become a contributing member of the team. The notes are not a snapshot of what is being said but an ongoing comparative analysis of positions and language used by each delegate since the beginning of the conference, with a column, titled 'Rose', presumably left open for further comparisons with the sessions of the other areas and communication beyond the confines of the conference. All these nuances are lost on her and the effort to think in that way; to make those subtle connections, seems to her simply impossible.

She welcomes the shift of her mind's attention from the content of the discussion to an abstract sensation of the room. The conference host is not among the participants, so the sounds are monotone, despite the jumps between languages and overplayed moments of indignation that break the overall flow. The visual content is much more interesting, thanks to a pyramid-shaped skylight directly above the table. Lines from the skylight frame slowly cross and recross the delegates, telling a complex story of the time that passes. The restrained, professional movements of the delegates, out of time with the imperious shadowed hands, give the clock face a faintly defiant animation.

The image gives Cesarine a sense of passive separation, similar to when she first heard about the conference on the radio. She can be a simple spectator for a moment, even though she knows that it cannot last. She thinks that maybe she should follow the ideas of Lucien and view the scene as magical. She could put more distance between herself and the world if she cut the fantastical interpretation her mind was creating from its mundane underpinnings, underpinnings only complex due to their number and the intricacy of their interconnections. She wonders if she isn't doing that anyway. The meanings of words frequently pass her by unabsorbed, just as much listening to the radio as following the flow of the conference host and ignoring the discussion directly in front of her at the moment.

Her imagination pre-empts whatever decision she might have made and the distance closes quickly. The cause of the restricted movements of the delegates becomes clear, despite their elaborate costumes; all of them share Valery's wooden composition, with limbs attached by crude joints with limited play. The constraints make the virtuosity of each gesture all the more impressive, reminiscent of the best work at the National School of Puppetry. Cesarine turned her back on that virtuosity, a practiced mastery with a long history, to embrace the awkwardness of new forms.

Perhaps 'awkwardness' should be replaced by 'absurdity'. Now that she has read some of the fictionalized accounts of life and protest similar to those in the old country, she has a better sense of why some of the most difficult – and comic – aspects of life before the defection did not affect her. She had always been aware of the absurdity of the daily reminder on the radio that shoes could be bought at the shoe store and, if the news included a segment on how the price of some good was going to be stable, that it was time to stock up as the price was about to go up. On those days, she had waited in the interminable lines along with everyone else.

She did not, however, think that those announcements were entirely absurd. They were just a mechanical reminder of how one was supposed to act publicly. There never seemed to be any expectation that the information was to be believed, let alone be taken as gospel. They were more along the lines of programs she has listened to since that take a moment to note the official time so people can set their watches. It doesn't matter if the time is correct or objective or even sensible; it is about coordination, not content. This doesn't mean that satirizing the content isn't amusing, it just doesn't seem important.

So, even if Cesarine can't pick up the nuances of diplomatic discourse that become frustratingly evident once Etienne has written them down, the obvious way to find something to contribute is to focus on what is actually being communicated; to view the mechanics as significant only insofar as they relate to content. This is a far-more-reasonable goal, even if it represents a great deal of what she despises. It will be like extending the hour-long classes on esthetics from the university to cover an entire day, only without the hope of seriously influencing the outcome. The people at the table have heads of solid wood; there is not a single musical instrument among them.

She leans towards Etienne to take another glance at his notebook. He notices and shifts so that she can easily see what he is writing. She puts an effort into taking in the notebook as best as she can without being overwhelmed. The word at the nexus of most of the connections is 'border'. Etienne has linked each country's understanding of borders in relation to people, documents, art, information, ideas, etc. in addition to security, economy and definitions of 'state'. The last three are mostly blank, waiting for input from Rose.

Focusing on one word and picking up on what is being said around it seems doable to Cesarine. She layers sound onto the visual spectacle, represses her distaste for off-kilter and jumpy rhythms, and waits for a cue. 'Frontier' is the first word that draws her attention. East Germany hammers the point of the inviolability of frontiers as they currently exist. Valery and others accept the notion while questioning the 'iron'-like nature of the borders between East and West. Recognizing the line, they argue, does not imply that they accept its impermeability. Etienne quickly flips back a couple of pages, and then a couple more, to give Cesarine a glimpse showing that the East German delegate has used the exact same language before, making the same point repeatedly. She gathers from the notes that the context is quite different each time and that the point never quite fits, but he flipped back too quickly for her to be sure.

Although Cesarine could theoretically shed some light on the situation in East Germany, she is relieved that it is not one of the countries, like her own, on which she is the putative expert. As she scans the pages, she cannot find references to countries similar to her own in Etienne's notebook. Despite the fact that it will further undermine whatever is left of her illusion of expertise, she resolves to ask Etienne about it during the break.

"The popular opinion is that, since it was not that long ago that the Soviets invaded and the central committee of the party was replaced, they didn't have the time or inclination to develop an independent voice. If the Soviet position was unwavering, they would likely be loudly parroting it. With other countries, like Poland, in the mix though, the Soviet strategy has become ever so slightly erratic. So, staying discrete seems to be their best option.

"It is obviously very different for East Germany, since the border between the two Germanys is one of the most important drivers for holding this conference in the first place. The only thing that was recognized after the war was the boundaries of the four administrative areas; the British, French and American that make up West Germany, and the Soviet area that makes up the East. Most of the international community does not recognize the existence of two Germanys. If the border is recognized as a line between countries, it follows that there must be different countries on either side. By enshrining the line in an international treaty, the signatories are bound to accept the countries."

Etienne pauses before continuing.

"You know, I was really impressed with how you were concentrating on the table in there. I mean, I imagine that it is old hat for you. In my world, it is pretty rare. Diplomats come into rooms like these with strict instructions from their government and little discretion, so make a habit of not getting too involved in the discussion. This conference has the potential of being a bit different, since there are far more participants and will likely take too long for the politicians to keep it as a priority. But, habits being what they are...

"Anyway, a long time ago a friend of mine mentioned to me that most students in his drawing classes drew badly because they focused too much attention on the paper and not enough on the model. Some students glanced at the model at the beginning of the session, and then seemed to completely forget that it was there. I thought that it was so strange, and then I saw a roomful of fellow foreign-service students do the same thing in a mock session.

"Of course, the context is important too. My notes can be pretty hard to decipher without a lot of other information. We will go over it, see how much I missed, what you can add and get input from Valery and Rose. It is just so easy to get caught up in the context, in the information; to start constructing theories based on how Romania has presented itself historically; and completely miss who she is today. It may be second nature to you but, for me, it was refreshing to see someone really paying attention."

If only I had something to show for it, Cesarine thinks.

Still, now she wishes that she had her esthetics students with her. She could then give them a real-life example of a pragmatically esthetic experience, where a person intentionally struggles with an environment with which they are at odds, that they don't fully grasp, in order to come into harmony with it. What she likes about the example is that neither the initial environment, nor the harmonized one is art. It is also unlikely that Etienne would ever consider himself an artist just because he approaches his work with certain esthetic sensibilities.

It does not bother her that he completely misinterpreted what she had been paying attention to. These sorts of misunderstandings are, after all, an almost daily occurrence in her life. She can try to focus more on the delegates from her country and others like them. She has a sudden vision of Canadian trappers when she thinks of the Czechoslovak delegates and curses Lucien under her breath. They have been mostly silent, so they shouldn't be as overwhelming as the others. At the same time, their forced orthodoxy means that there is little hope that any of her eventual insights will be helpful for arriving at her delegation's goals. She is filled with a weird mix of relief and irrelevance at the idea that, even useful, her contribution will likely be useless.

She walks back into the room with Etienne. Her idea is to build off what she has already imagined. This is not like the boxes in the backroom that have to be organized in such a way as to be accessible to everyone. Her insights can be more opaque than Etienne's notes are to her, so long as she can link them after the fact to what she has been reading or the observations of others in the group when she shares them. It should be simple enough to study the physical reactions of the wooden puppets at the table, perhaps compare them to classic figures. For dramatic reasons, she would like to see a resemblance between a delegate and Don Juan, and to see him ultimately dragged off to Hell. That, though, would be getting ahead of herself.

Everyone settles in, noticeably faster this time. Cesarine scans the delegates and is about to focus on the few she thinks she should concentrate on when she is distracted by a woman sitting behind the representative from her old country. The woman is staring directly at her, analyzing her in a manner completely opposite to an esthetic experience. The look is entirely mechanical, stripped of emotional intent. There isn't even a touch of curiosity or the cold antipathy instinctively felt towards a known traitor.

Cesarine, in contrast, is almost shaking with giddiness. On some basic level, her mind has already labeled the woman as a likely threat. The warning is completely drowned out, though, by the instinctive conviction that this person is as close as one can possibly come to the ideal mechanical being. Cesarine closes her eyes, grips the arms of her chair tightly and breathes as evenly as possible, so as to not give in to the urge to run across the room. When she reopens her eyes, the woman is gone and Etienne is glancing askance at her, in between looking at the table and his notebook. Her giddiness falls to a profound sense of loss. She tries to concentrate on the delegates at the table, but can only see their limitations. The virtuosity, the nuances that would differentiate a Don Juan from a Don Philippe, is completely lost.

Chapter 7

"You must be the famous 'Sorceress'," Coralie says as she opens the door for Cesarine to enter. "When Lucien told me that he had finally met the Sorceress, I confess that I had absolutely no idea who he was referring to. When he explained, I was concerned. Still am, really."

"Ah. Why is that?" Cesarine responds, making an effort to not be overcome with apathy over Lucien's domestic issues. She should actually be interested, insofar as they are a distraction from the mechanical woman. The sole reason for accepting Lucien's invitation to a dinner he is hosting for friends was to take her mind off that moment and the frustration that has followed.

Cesarine has forced herself to continue with her reading and try to absorb what she can from sessions and team strategy meetings. The hope that she will see the mechanical woman again has lasted far longer than it should have, given that she has completely disappeared from the center. Cesarine's curiosity has not diminished, but rather seems to be bolstered by the frustration. She has spent her life playing with the mechanics – real and imaginary – of objects, so when she comes across someone who typifies, in a sense, her life's work, it is difficult to just let go. Without letting go, concentrating on other things is an uphill battle.

"Oh, it is nothing against you personally. I love Lucien to death; he is just not the most constant of all people. He finds it difficult to stick with his work, to follow through. To see him fixated on something that stops him from even beginning..."

Coralie shrugs as she enters the salon, Cesarine following. Neither blend with the small group of excessively well-, though casually dressed, young men.

"Of course," Coralie adds loud enough for everyone to hear,

"everyone here is a bad influence on him, so it doesn't much matter."

"We've been unmasked!" one of the group exclaims.

"I think Lucien is the bad influence, what with his starry-eyed poetics and, wait, is that his anti-muse?" another adds.

"Well, so long as she didn't bring any of her kryptonite here."

"Are you implying that Lucien is Superman?"

"He is an alien."

"I have always suspected."

"Don't they put subliminal messages in movies in Russia?"

"A message that silenced one of our most mediocre talents. The bastards! What will they think of next?"

"Now I have to step in," Lucien finally says. "What is this about calling me a talent? That just isn't right. No, the message was to assassinate the prime minister. How could I not be at a loss for words; kill someone who falls asleep at his own press conferences? Such misdirected violence."

"He does look so peaceful."

"It's a bit of a boy's club, as you can see," Coralie explains to Cesarine. "The tragedy is that the people who could be a positive influence are too busy with their own work to actually influence. When they do show up, they are so preoccupied that they suck the energy from the room. So, we are stuck with this lot."

"Right, introductions!" Lucien calls out. "Cesarine, the Lumière sister of the animation world, this is Henry, Jack, Eugene and Raoul. They all have some connection to journalism, though it is too long, complicated and, frankly, tedious to get into. And of course you have met Coralie, my better eight tenths. It fluctuates."

"It is nice to meet you all," Cesarine says, finding a place to sit. She only saw the mechanical woman for a moment. It could have been an illusion; a vision of what she yearned for in an environment filled with classical wooden figures. It is not as if she was able to walk over, flip back the ear hatch and take a look inside.

"So, about those subliminal images?" Raoul asks as he pours Cesarine a glass of wine from one of the unmarked bottles scattered across the space.

"Thank you. I kept it simple, just a nudge to convince the audience that they liked what they saw. And even that got out of control. All this talk about sorceresses and wizardry... I put the word 'magic' in the mix one time and now it's all people think about."

"I would have gone all *Nineteen Eighty-Four*, redefining words to shape a new reality," Henry offers.

"They add that before it is broadcast on TV," Jack points out.

"Not really," Cesarine says, thinking after the fact that it would be better if she stayed silent. She wants the group to keep its comic tone; she could use a humorous backdrop that undercuts her overly serious reflections. She fears that her contributions will weigh down the conversation.

"But it has been proven."

"I can only speak for small countries like the one I am from, but people live too close to the borders. There is no way to block emissions from areas outside the government's control. Orwell's vision only works as well as it did – which was far from perfectly – because his world was split into three massive countries." She can't help herself, but at least it is distracting. It would be great if the group would break out into song, like a chorus from a light-hearted operetta. It would be even better if such an obvious observation could be a respectable contribution to her delegation.

"Then why don't people revolt?" Henry asks.

"They don't know any better," Eugene offers. "Same reason that they read your articles."

"But Cesarine's point is that they do know better."

"I'll rephrase: even if readers understand that there is a higher-quality newspaper available at a store a couple of blocks further or at a slightly higher cost, they don't make the connection between effort or money invested and a better life. So, they content themselves with your drivel."

"Sounds like laziness or being cheap," Raoul says.

"Sounds like someone is bitter," Henry adds.

"It's the Gandhi problem," Lucien says as he heads into the kitchen to check on the food. Everyone is silent until he reappears a moment later.

"This isn't my theory. It is from an article I read once. A journalist from across the wall read a biography of Gandhi and wondered to himself, first of all, why the book was even available and, then, why people did not take inspiration from it and be proactive in changing the system. His country had seen its fair share of Soviet tanks, just like Cesarine's, so she can tell me if I have it wrong. He was under the impression that the reason tanks in the capital worked so well was that there was never sufficient popular support for the demonstrations. He concluded that people were just too well off; it was far from India's rampant poverty. Though things were bad, they could always imagine much worse. Holding on to what they had was too important."

All eyes turn to Cesarine, who is busy making mental notes. She had not participated in the demonstrations that led to the invasion of her country, nor was she part of the artistic underground following the crackdown. Her knowledge is limited to vague ideas of what triggered the protests and where the hot spots were, mainly so that she could avoid them the few times she left her workshop at a reasonable hour.

"It isn't all that different from here, then?" she asks.

"Well, we do vote," Jack points out.

"Speak for yourself," Eugene says.

"I don't vote either," Coralie admits.

"And you call us a bad example," Henry jokingly chastises her.

"Jack's the outlier," Raoul says. "Let's take a moment to feel guilty about letting down our society. At least it'll give us another reason to drink."

"And that's a good thing?" Jack asks.

"Coralie can defend herself," Henry says.

"But she does need support," Eugene adds.

"Don't we all?" Coralie asks.

"You are premiering tomorrow. None of us are under that sort of pressure."

"Premiering?" Cesarine queries, content that the conversation has moved to lighter terrain and away from anything one might assume that she has knowledge of.

"A play," Coralie explains.

"You are the director, an actress?"

"A diva," Eugene declares.

"That would require singing," Coralie says. "I am playing the lead."

"What play?" Cesarine asks as Lucien heads back into the kitchen.

"'Phaedra', if you know it."

"Yes, somewhat. I left the classics behind after school."

"Most people did, I think. Which is bizarre because most of them were pretty crazy and tragic; that sort of thing usually attracts people in droves."

"It still can," Lucien says as he comes back into the room. "All you need is some good press, something that will work against the flaccid excuse of a marketing campaign."

"Jack and I got the assignment," Raoul notes. "We already flipped a coin: I will be against it, he will find it wonderful. We'll stir up enough controversy to make it a must see."

"Do you have an extra ticket?" Eugene asks.

"I already sold my spares. The theatre was generous in the number they gave out, but priorities are priorities."

"Sorry, I sold mine too," Jack adds. "Thus, the scotch." He points to the unopened bottle in the middle of the table.

"I do feel that I am getting the shaft from the foreign-service beat," Lucien says.

"Maybe if you wrote articles they would accept," Coralie suggests.

"Bah," Eugene says. "Anytime we have to compete with the international news agencies, we are bound to lose."

"For straight-up news, anyway," Raoul adds. "Unfortunately, the controversy usually writes itself in international news. The ideologies are well-entrenched, everyone has already picked sides and officials from all sides happily push everyone else's buttons when it suits them."

"And that's to say nothing about how anal they are about controlling press access," Jack says. "Even if we wanted to do a good job, it is almost impossible to get a soundbite that a hundred other reporters don't hear at the same time."

"What bugs me," Lucien complains, "is the waste of food. At every break, the organizers pile food on the table in the central hall. The delegates barely touch it. Then the staff cart it away, without even asking if the shadows on the wall want a bite. I imagine that the serious, foreign types would be too dignified to eat the scraps, but some of us aren't dignified, damn it."

"No, no you aren't," everyone agrees.

Cesarine feels one step behind, and belatedly asks no one in particular, "Why don't you push their buttons when it doesn't suit them?"

"We really should," Jack responds. "But it is either not worth the risk or is not very sporting."

"Or not very profitable," Eugene adds.

"Or not at all interesting," Lucien says. "With Coralie's play, a review can make a big difference. Will writing, say, that the populations in the East are so attached to material wealth that they can't even be bothered to protest change anything? Will it make them seem less alien to equally materialistic people here? Not that I want to discount our need to eat and buy scotch, you understand."

"For a moment, I was going to say that you should give up and go back to poetry," Eugene says.

"Why doesn't he write a play?" Cesarine asks.

"Because we already have our hands full keeping Coralie's career afloat," Raoul replies. "And we actually like her."

"Thanks a lot!" Coralie exclaims sarcastically, before sighing. "Sometimes it is depressing how much the audience must be told what is good. Personal judgment be damned, they must learn what others think before daring to venture an opinion. It's even more depressing that what other people think ends up just being the position of some random reviewer in whatever newspaper is at hand."

"Wouldn't writing and reviewing a play mean more free tickets?" Cesarine continues, following the playful cynicism.

"This is a small town," Jack explains. "There is only so much interest we can drum up. If we can't offer a noticeable bump in sales, I can't imagine us seeing many tickets. Sometimes I think that we would do better in a bigger city."

"All we need to do is bridge the gap between the foreigners and the locals," Eugene argues. "There are plenty of theatres that are aimed at the steady stream of employees of the internationals, the multinationals and whatever other sort of group that decides to set up shop here. Yay, neutrality! First we have to get over the language barrier, then bypass the community outlets and then we should be set."

"That would be far more difficult than just moving; preferably to a place where almost everyone speaks the same language as us and at least a substantial minority gets our humor."

"I don't get our humor," Raoul says.

"That's because some of us try too hard to be clever," Eugene explains.

"Is that what it is?" Coralie asks, surprised. "Here I thought that it was just the lack of originality."

"Says the girl playing Phaedra."

"I for one think that..." Jack begins.

"No, no lectures; pastiche is not the highest form of art," Coralie cuts in.

"It blends the best parts..."

"It can, but then it can also combine all sorts of lowest common denominators, try to be all things to all people."

"Cesarine hasn't heard..."

"Then there is still hope for her."

"And here I was going to write you a glowing..."

"Don't pretend that the controversy isn't good for you too."

Jack sits back with an exaggerated pout. Then he realizes that his glass is empty, so sacrifices the effect to lean forward and reach for a bottle of wine.

"I'm surprised he didn't go for the scotch," Eugene says.

"All in good time," Jack replies as he pours the wine.

Lucien goes back into the kitchen.

"The food had better be ready soon," Raoul calls after him. "I'm famished."

"Just about there," Lucien calls back. "I couldn't have you taste such a gourmet meal completely sober."

"Wise man," Eugene says. "That's where I always go wrong. Everybody goes into critic mode; all pompousness and unrealistic expectations."

"We are doing a lot better at lowering our expectations when we eat at your place," Jack points out.

"Okay, dinner's ready," Lucien declares.

The group moves to the table; Coralie guiding Cesarine; everyone bringing glasses and bottles. Cesarine wonders if there is any order to how they are sitting, but has trouble assigning individual personalities to each of them. In her eyes, they have become the chorus she had more or less hoped for in the beginning. She had taken Lucien to be an idealist who grudgingly wrote articles to make ends meet, and so expected his friends to have a similar outlook. Instead, they come off as mercenary. Perhaps they are just worn down by the material realities of life, perhaps they are impatient to put their work out in, and be recognized by, the world.

As far as she knows, this attitude could be common among the people of her old country, especially after the invasion. If the Gandhi problem was real, it would make sense. It also would be more useful for her if she was attached to the economics sub-delegation and could pull off selling the ideas as original. All this leads her back to wallowing in her uselessness. Only now, self-deprecation seems to her quite pleasant relative to her fixation on the maddeningly illusive mechanical woman.

Chapter 8

The now-familiar cacophony of boxes and murmur of the speaker welcome Cesarine into the backroom. Her fixation has faded into a vague anxiety that she is able to push to the back of her mind, leaving space for internalizing some of the insights from her reading and Etienne-style observation of delegates. When she catches herself replaying the moment she saw the mechanical woman, she forces herself to imagine flaws in the mechanism. The penetrating stare feeds a brain composed of elements from an old bicycle bitten by road salt through a series of hard winters. The grinding of the gritty, unlubricated chain over worn, mismatched gear teeth is drowned out by the screeching of the heavily corroded chain links. The sense of awe is replaced by a mixture of horror and pity at such degradation. The illusion lacks the conviction of what she usually creates, but it is better than nothing.

Valery shows infinite patience, giving her opportunities for input in a way that avoids awkwardness when she is unable to take advantage of them. In his unguarded moments, Etienne lets an edge of disillusionment show through. His deep-seated conviction in the importance of keen observation is at odds with his increasingly obvious mistake regarding how she sees the world. Rose, who had tried to push her in the right direction at the outset – largely because she felt responsible for her presence – has come to dismiss her as imposed baggage. It was after all the ministry that instructed them to include a defector on the team. So long as Cesarine doesn't rearrange anything or become an obstacle in any other way, Rose can focus on what is truly important; providing Valery with the best intelligence possible so he has a higher chance of success in the negotiations.

Cesarine finds the indifference and the disillusionment comforting and would like nothing more than to continue to watch the interplay between the production line, the military headquarters and the block of wood, as she has come to do during the team meetings not overwhelmed by her fixation. She still feels the need to add something to the functional side though, and actually feels somewhat prepared to contribute something. Something useful, even if unlikely to spark much enthusiasm – let alone public effervescence.

"There is another soft spot on the East," Rose is explaining. "It seems that Hungary is getting tired of sending all the East Germans who go there to find an easier border to cross to the west back to their country. They aren't too vocal about it, but they aren't as cowed as the countries invaded in the 60s either."

"How do you think we can use it?" Valery asks.

"They could be more open to a freedom of movement clause being included in the final text. It would likely end up with the same 'national security' and 'public order' restrictions that are showing up everywhere, but would still give them cover if they decide to let their enforcement become more lax. In any case, 'free movement' is back on the table."

"We can connect that idea to a number of articles," Etienne adds. "Freedom of movement for scientific cooperation, cultural advancement, assembly and organization…"

"And it can be coordinated with the other areas; the economic area especially."

"It will also have to be run by the minister, since he thought that it was overly provocative in the area title," Valery says.

"And then he suddenly lost all interest in the process," Rose points out.

"Don't worry," Etienne says, "he'll be back near the end for the signing, photographs and second guessing."

Valery smiles. "When both of you look back on this conference in ten years' time, you will appreciate it for the opportunity it is. You will likely never have this much freedom from political interference and this much trust in diplomats again in your careers. However, that hinges on being proactive in briefings and other communication. Of course, if you prefer photo ops, it isn't that difficult to become a politician in a country as small as ours."

"I'll prepare a backgrounder for you," Rose says.

Valery moves on to the next item. "The agenda for the next session is focused on social and cultural development. Besides the link to freedom of movement, what are your thoughts?"

As Rose and Etienne turn to pertinent pages of their notes, Cesarine decides that it is time to speak.

"This might be too close to movement, but something should be said about not moving, of staying in place."

"Can you expand on that?" Valery asks.

Cesarine thinks of a variety of examples in the books she has just read of characters being assigned to live in places to break up groups of dissidents, because they don't fit societal norms in an overtly public way or to limit their interaction with foreigners. Her own experience is, as usual, lacking. Even expanding the notion of personal experience to fellow puppeteers, she can't come up with anything. The puppetry community she remembers could be a strange and sometimes subversive lot, but they never strayed far enough from cherished national traditions to be forcibly moved. Honestly, the only people who understood the subversion were the tiny minority who were deeply familiar with the folklore.

"I am sure that you are aware of the examples of members of the intelligentsia being assigned to other locations in the country to break up groups that the government finds troublesome. It was fairly rare in the animation community – more common among scientists and writers, I suppose – but it did happen occasionally. Being cut off like that was not helpful for social and cultural development."

"That's a good point," Rose says. "The Soviets have Gorky for whenever they need to keep people and projects away from prying eyes. And that is different than sending someone to a GULAG, which has a legal – even if specious – process attached to it."

"We have records of professors being reassigned from Prague to Bratislava for those sorts of reasons," Etienne adds. "I think that it is more closely tied to movement than development though, so we should aim to have the point added to the former rather than the latter. We will get some clear support for development if it is left simple, but there is no way that that will last if we complicate the article."

"Which countries do you have in mind?" Valery asks.

"Poland and Romania," Rose and Etienne say at the same time.

"Both are aiming for an identity independent from Russia," Etienne explains, "which will require a certain amount of self-determination on an individual, human level. I don't see them going from there to the freedom of an individual to live where they want."

"Okay," Valery says. "Rose, can you work with Cesarine to add, say, the freedom to choose where one resides, to the movement backgrounder?"

"Sure," Rose replies.

Cesarine is not sure whether her idea was actually constructive, or whether the team had just defaulted to supportive mode out of surprise that she said anything at all. The negative side of the inner workings of the team is that they are either solid and opaque or well enough put together to not be affected by emotional tremors. The only thing to do for now is to look for another opportunity, though she hopes that Rose will bluntly tell her the truth later.

"As for development, it has become more controversial since the beginning," Valery says. "Some delegates have been claiming that it is a capitalist wedge, given how central it is to Western ideology. I don't really see it, since the main argument for centrally controlled production is that it leads to better, which is to say more equitable, development. In any case, Etienne stumbled on to the expression that we will likely use going forward: 'self-determination'."

"So, we are dropping 'development' completely?" Rose asks.

"I don't think we can. No, it will just be under the rubric of self-determination. That way, development won't be seen as having intrinsic value, but rather will be a means to something everyone can accept. There are still questions, of course; notably whether self-determination is for persons or peoples."

"It would have to be for peoples," Etienne argues. "Otherwise we will get similar pushback by the anti-development crowd for being too pro-individual."

"We shouldn't have a problem with that though," Rose adds, "since social and cultural development is by nature a group activity. So long as individual rights, state obligations against discrimination and the like are included elsewhere in the document."

Cesarine debates whether to challenge the notion that cultural development is necessarily a group activity. She quickly finds herself stuck with a series of distastefully philosophical questions: when does an object created by a member – particularly a marginal member – of a society or culture become a cultural object? At what point did the animations she created in the old country become a part of the country's culture? Did that change when she decided that she no longer wanted to be part of that society, taking into account that she was completely marginal when she lived there? Which people has profited from her work for their self-determination since her defection?

Rose seems to read her mind: "Now that I think about it, we need to ensure that an individual's freedom of expression captures things like art. It would be strange to reduce stuff like Cesarine's films to an expression of a people, taking the artist out of the equation, and I don't see the anti-discrimination clause really covering that."

Cesarine chooses to see her work used as an example as a positive sign. She would like to add something to the discussion to reinforce her presence, but is once more at a loss. The problem with what she has read is that it is always from the perspective of one or a number of individuals. Books that touched on the war frequently dealt with how approximate the relation was between the identity of German or Hungarian with individual ambitions or quirks. This group-versus-individual struggle evolved into the communist ideal for everyone versus the party's incapacity to accept humanizing qualities like humor. After the Soviet invasions and normalizations, books tended to view group identity as a running joke of questionable taste, reminiscent of the good soldier Švejk. None of this is particularly inspiring for attributing rights to peoples.

"We negotiated the freedom of expression article a while ago," Valery says, flipping through a sheaf of paper to find the wording the table had agreed on.

"We're good; it included art," Etienne says, having found the passage first.

Cesarine leans over to look at Etienne's notebook to see if art is singled out. She is at first pleasantly surprised to see 'any other media' included in the pertinent clause. Her work would be covered even if it was stripped of its erroneous label. Then the realization hits her in the gut that the wording was decided during the session when she saw the mechanical woman.

All she can see is her – she is not sure anymore how best to describe her. The woman is kneeling in front of the chair across the room, surrounded by neat rows of tools and parts. Her head is sitting on the chair, detached from her body, oriented so that the eyes can continue to bore into Cesarine. Cesarine stares, fascinated, as every worn-down part her imagination had conceived is methodically replaced, then carefully adjusted and lubricated. She lacks the will to rein her imagination in, to give it new instructions, to do anything at all. The shadows from the skylight frame inexorably mark the movement of the sun, accentuating the vertiginous sensation of reversal that strips away all the progress Cesarine has made to overcome this obsession.

Cesarine feels a hand on her shoulder. The image fades as she looks around to see that she is alone with Rose and the incessantly talkative files.

"Good contribution to the discussion," Rose says. "I hope that it was the first of many. Let's put together the piece on the freedom to reside where one wishes, shall we?"

Cesarine nods, relieved that she was able pass through the vision without drawing undue attention to herself. The relief is fleeting, giving away to a hollow ache in the pit of her stomach where the realization first hit her.

Chapter 9

As Cesarine makes her way to the backroom with Etienne after a session, she senses a change in the sea of people in the main hall. Instead of passing anonymously through the crowd, she feels curious eyes on her and voices lowered to whispers at her approach. It would be like the audience at a festival featuring her work, only nobody seems to want to directly interact with her. She finds herself hoping that a large vessel would pass and draw all the attention, but her desire proves as ineffectual as Lucien's when he tried to will a clash between the two grand phalanxes.

"Why is everyone looking at us?" she asks Etienne.

"Hmm, don't know," Etienne replies without looking up from his notebook. He is still jotting down notes and linking ideas while his observations are still fresh. She continues to be surprised that he doesn't run into anything or anyone, with all the miniature soldiers in his head analyzing the map in the middle of the headquarters in light of new reconnaissance reports and no one observing the field directly in front of them.

Etienne finally looks up once they are installed at the backroom table.

"You don't have anything to add?" he asks.

Cesarine has taken to joining him in looking over his notes and making suggestions as to connections or nuances that he might have missed. Generally she has nothing to add, so she just compliments him on details that he has picked out. Either way, she continues to learn a lot from his approach.

"Sorry, I was distracted. It was like we were the center of attention in the hall, and not in a good way."

Valery enters at that moment.

"Do you know a Léon Chaulieu, by any chance?" he asks Cesarine.

"I know of him. He was a highly respected novelist in the old country before the invasion. His books disappeared after that, so I imagine that his work was banned. Why?"

"It's not yet authenticated, but an issue of an underground newspaper with his name all over it has mysteriously appeared everywhere. There is an article on you, which, as far as I can see, is the only thing that is of any interest. You should read it. Oh, and the appearance is not at all mysterious: certain people from your old country seem to have taken exception to seeing you here."

Valery hands Cesarine a thin sheaf of A4-sized paper, stapled at the top left corner, open to the article in question:

Get your copies of Cesarine Vatsulka's films while you can, for she is no longer among us! Or, don't. It is probably not worth the trouble. I haven't seen many of them, though I have it on good authority that they are on the whole brilliant; at the very sharpest end of bleeding edge. Some grumble that the narrative is sacrificed to innovative technique. Those criticisms, I understand, only arise a week or two after the viewing, when the wonder has worn off.

So, why is it not worth the trouble? You are already reading a not entirely legal article, so it now being illegal to possess them shouldn't stop you. Most of them are only available on movie reels, so that could be an issue. It would be a challenge to set up a screening.

None of that justifies such a sweeping assertion. Setting up a screening could be simplicity itself for many of you. For others, technical innovation without an at least equal advancement in story-telling could be of no interest at all. I would not want to presume.

The door opens and Rose enters.

"It has been authenticated," she announces. "However, it is from eight years ago. Apparently he is still putting out issues.

They are distributed informally among the underground artistic community in the capital. For some reason, he always sends a copy to the government, so they would have had it on hand for an occasion like this. It is a bit strange that they would use it in its original form though, since, while it does undermine Cesarine, it doesn't exactly portray them in a better light."

Cesarine continues to read the article:

I do have a weakness, though; I cannot completely detach a work from the choices of its creator. I have nothing negative to say about what I have seen of Vatsulka's work. I think that it is misguided to expect them to be epics that dramatically explore the full range of the human condition. Conversely, Vatsulka's profound selfishness is, I believe, relevant.

For many years now, there has been a regular stream of people who have chosen to abandon our country. Most of these people, from tradespeople, through academics to musicians, have one point in common. They, or a close member of their family, cannot freely practice their vocation. Some are denied a post at a university, others membership in a guild. If there are children involved, a child was denied a place at a school. Alternatively, they are pushed by the authorities to a point where their vocation takes over their lives; it becomes a sickness that threatens to bring them to an untimely end.

Cesarine Vatsulka was able to pursue her animation freely. She was supported yet not interfered with by the government. Many writers cannot publish, numerous musicians and actors cannot perform. A retrospective of Vatsulka's work was closed recently only because she left. A projection of new films was scheduled for early fall. One of the reasons she was able to slip away so easily is that she was completely free to attend international festivals that featured her animation.

She was in no way oppressed. She did not use her freedom

to help someone who was. There is no evidence that she cared about politics or about the state of society. I would say that she was not even aware that her work enriched the lives of people around her. Now we are all worse off. There will be no more open screenings of her work.

Vatsulka is very talented. She will likely find personal glory in the West that would be impossible here. She will also find more variety on grocery-store shelves. For that, she has turned her back on a supportive community. Her films are unquestionably important. Her egoism has made it difficult to view them. Given that, it is not worth the risk to seek them out.

Cesarine's first reaction is to appreciation that Chaulieu did not refer to her as an artist, or to her work as art. Then, she wonders what his reaction would be in learning that she ended up, more or less by her own design, as a professor at an obscure animation school in a small provincial city of a rather unremarkable country. She is still appreciative of the variety available in the local grocery stores, though.

Rose and Etienne are busy analyzing the text and the motivations of the delegation of Cesarine's old country using the information Rose brought and the resources they have on hand. Valery observes Cesarine, increasingly amused by her lack of reaction.

"What do you think?" Valery asks as Cesarine hands the newspaper back to him.

Cesarine shrugs. "It's true enough." She wonders if Valery is hoping that the article sparks more ideas from her, perhaps as a knee-jerk reaction against the assertion of profound selfishness. She could after all still do some good for the community she was supposed to have been part of. However, the last thing she wants to do is raise expectations.

"It seems to me that the majority of defectors are labeled as selfish traitors at one point or another."

"I suppose so."

"You didn't play much of role in the community the article refers to, did you?"

"None of the puppetry people were very involved."

"But you went well beyond puppetry."

"Only in the technical sense, as Chaulieu wrote. My animation does not engage with the struggles of our time, let alone the human condition in a larger sense."

"You do yourself a disservice in cutting technical innovation from society and culture. It's a bit of a tautology these days, but technology does increasingly define how we live, how we interact with each other."

"Sure. The relation between the two is probably unavoidable; perhaps my focus on technology hampered my ability to connect to other creative people in a more direct and organic way. It is difficult to see how the isolation was different than that resulting from the dedication to the rarified world of classic storytelling typical among my peers. The only real difference is that stop-motion animation was far more time-intensive. While others were discussing politics in cafés or protesting in the streets, I was in my workshop, preoccupied with regular cyclical movements of angular rocks in a character's brain at twenty-four shots a second.

"Insofar as my intentions matter, I never had the intention of exploring the relationship between technology and humanity."

Cesarine cringes at what she just said; intentionality is just as annoying a philosophical rabbit hole as nature.

"All that aside, how do you think this should be handled?" she asks, trying to change the direction of the conversation.

"Are there any skeletons in your closet that the vetting did not catch?"

"No."

"Then we do nothing. It is probably just a flash in the pan. We figured that there would be some fallout sooner or later when we included you in the delegation. If the worst that they have to throw at us is that you are selfish, then I think we should count ourselves lucky."

"I have an idea," Rose says. "Why don't we encourage a local cinema to show some of Cesarine's films? The article focuses on how great her work is and how selfish she is. If we nudge people's attention towards her art, all the rest will seem far less important. Plenty of great artists were complete assholes, pardon my French, and yet all was somehow forgiven just because they were considered great."

"I get the impression sometimes that well-adjusted artists are about as common as unicorns," Etienne adds. "Present company excluded, of course."

"Can you handle following a tight script?" Valery asks Cesarine.

"I suppose so," Cesarine replies after a moment of hesitation.

"You don't have to."

"What would you want me to say?"

"I like Rose's idea of making your animation available. However, it has to be your idea. No matter how many great artists happen to be selfish assholes, you can't be both one of them and a member of this delegation. The very fact that you decided to join us to help improve people's lives across Europe – including your old country – is proof that you are anything but egotistical. That you are in a better position to make a difference after you left shows that it was the best choice under the circumstances. And while you unfortunately aren't in the position to influence the government's decision to censor your work back home, you would like to make it easier for those who might want to see some examples, by setting up a screening here and by fighting for the free movement of art across the continent, regardless of borders.

"We will have to tone it down a bit; make it less aggressive, avoid political pitfalls, that sort of thing. We also have to make sure that it serves the domestic audience as much, if not more, than the foreign one. Despite the idea of including someone like you on the team originally coming from the ministry, they have been waffling ever since. We can use the screening to clearly establish that you are an asset for the team."

"That was a quick change from doing nothing," Rose observes.

"You and Etienne were very convincing."

"What happens if we change our minds? After all, if the article is a flash in the pan, as you suggested; it will be buried pretty quickly under all the other rumors and revelations that circulate around here. And, there would be less chance that something would go wrong."

Cesarine prefers doing nothing, but does not consider a projection of her work and the usual lies that go along with it to be much of a burden. Pretending to be altruistic seems to her to have more in common with playing the role of artist than it does with contributing to the team's strategy. She still can't shake the ache in the pit of her stomach; if anything, it has matured into a ball of anxiety. She smiles slightly as the idea that all of these can be rolled up into her 'A' game crosses her mind.

She suspects that Rose is right; Valery has another reason for changing his mind, though she doubts that he will come out and say it. On some level, her pretending to be useful could actually be useful. She just can't put her finger on why, especially since the freedom of movement of ideas, art and all the rest has already been agreed to. More broadly, Valery has avoided mixing external influences – particularly those of the government – with the negotiations at the table. The article does change things, but not enough to explain such a public, media-oriented move. Not knowing also doesn't trouble her overly much; she doubts that she will ever be fully up to speed with what is going on around her.

"It is the best option from a purely international-relations standpoint," Valery says. "This conference is going to last a while, though, so we should think of how things look back home. An easily understood soundbite highlighting the importance of what we are doing can't hurt."

"Won't that bring attention from the government?" Rose asks. "I mean, we are committed to see the conference through to the end, so I am not sure what we are gaining here. Of course, that doesn't mean that I don't want to counter such an obvious attempt to weaken the team. We just need to be smart about it, is what I am saying."

"The freedom of movement bit is the smart part," Etienne says. "Correct me if I am wrong, but by saying that we are fighting for a clause that is already set to be included in the final document, the minister can claim a double win – recruiting Cesarine and getting the clause – without doing anything. Since he already doesn't want to be directly involved, so long as we give him a neatly wrapped-up package, he won't look further. We will have to invite him to the screening, to which he will most likely respond by asking the head of the delegation or Valery to attend in his place."

"So, you don't see a downside?" Rose asks.

"Sure; nobody could come. It could be seen as legitimizing Cesarine's defection, which no one from the East would want to be a part of. And those from the West, except perhaps the U.S. delegation, would want to give offense and risk making the negotiations more difficult than they already are. That's why this has to be Cesarine's initiative, in the most non-political way as possible. Essentially, she would need to approach a non-partisan local cinema and suggest to the manager that, if they wanted to show some of her work, she could be in attendance to answer audience questions. It would only be outside the building after the event that she would answer the more sensitive questions, and only if reporters bring them up first."

"Are you are okay with all that?" Rose asks Cesarine.

"I have hosted one or two screenings before," Cesarine responds. "Some of the most enjoyable have been with an audience of two or three people."

"It's settled, then," Valery says. "Now let's go over what happened in today's session."

Chapter 10

At Lucien's suggestion, Cesarine approaches the manager of a small, two-screen movie theatre just off the main boulevard. He had explained that it usually showed a variety of popular and art-house fare and held semi-regular retrospectives. It was one of the places he had seen her animation before, attracted, as he said, like the proverbial moth to the flame. The manager is initially delighted, but, after learning that she does not have any new work to offer, readjusts his reaction to moderately excited. He is of the opinion that a one-evening event would go over well and is confident that both rooms could be filled. A run is out of the question, though, without new material. They decide on showing fifteen shorts on one screen and a feature on the other, and then flipping them. All the other details quickly fall into place; just as Cesarine has done this sort of thing a couple of times before, this is not exactly the first time for the manager.

The night before the event, Cesarine settles in to go over the final talking points that she had worked on with Rose and Etienne one more time. She makes the mistake of imagining the potential crowd, which leads her to envision the mechanical woman, almost lost in the audience. The people around her slowly yet inexorably fall into the rhythm of the animation on the screen. Facial expressions evolve with regularity along disparate axes; some approaching awe, others amusement, boredom or distaste. Shifts of weight and coughs are unconsciously coordinated across the room with hints from the film that a moment where such sounds would not be overly disruptive is about to arrive. Mouthfuls of popcorn and sugary drinks fuel the machine, accelerating when the movie's energy increases, when even the inner workings of inanimate objects become frenetic.

The mechanical woman is divorced from this system. She is aware of it, plays with it with incongruous actions that throw off the people sitting directly next to her. The miscues emanate from her like a wave, giving the sense that she is not at all lost in the crowd, but the center of it. The waves crash against the screen, distorting the film for the audience, who can only see it refracted through the mist. The rhythm is altered, then altered again as the reaction from the distorted film meets the diffusion of another dissonant action. The tension initially creates a dramatic fervor that Cesarine has never witnessed in an audience. Without progression or resolution, however, the excitement surrounding the conflict wanes quickly. When the animation – one of the shortest of the group – comes to an end, the audience slumps in their chairs, exhausted. Cesarine looks back to where the mechanical woman is seated; she has, predictably enough, slipped away.

Through the projection, Cesarine was standing, frozen, in the wings, incapable of seeing what was on the screen. She was familiar enough with the film to know what the audience was reacting to, at least until the dissonance began. As she lost her points of reference, she tried in vain to force her body to move so she could see what the audience was watching. Once more, her imagination was betraying her, perhaps having decided that she was no longer a worthy director.

The refracted animation was not the only thing she yearned for her imaginary body to let her see. The mechanical woman was but an outline in the darkened auditorium. Cesarine sensed though that her idol did not stop at perfecting the bicycle drive-train in her head, but rather had somehow adapted it to multiply its functionality while refining its elegance. Her inability to move would usually not be a problem; inner workings have always been figments of her imagination with an at-most tenuous relation with reality. During the short, though, all that came to her was a flat, featureless area of darkness.

Her ball of anxiety has turned out to be more like a seed or cocoon. It cracked open during her dream, letting loose a flurry of curiosity and dread. After the maddening immobility, she did not even try to push the sensations back to the pit of her stomach. Instead, she ineffectually cursed them and hoped that the insanity wouldn't last.

By the end, the curiosity is at a similar level to what she felt when she first took up animation, but the sensation is completely different. It was always absurd on a certain level; there is no other way to describe trees full of gears that one could contemplate through a series of handy view ports, and that is to say nothing about the manipulation of time and spatial relations that she played with at a grand scale. She wanted to be the mechanical woman; to be able to take off her head, flip a hatch and poke around inside. The curiosity was about creating a world where that sort of thing would be commonplace, to go as far as her imagination could take her, given the techniques and materials available. The ambition was not to observe nature, mix in some passion and arrive at something innovative yet fundamentally the same, but rather to cut out chunks of nature and replace them wholesale. Pedantically, it is not as if she could ever create anything categorically different, but she really didn't care.

She can't remember if she actually wanted her dwindling curiosity to be topped up, or whether she was content to go gently into that good night. Given her penchant for fatalism, she is still not entirely sure why she joined the delegation and abandoned a life bereft of both personal and public effervescence. She had certainly not given a thought to the potential positive impacts of the conference on the artistic community of the old country until Valery mentioned it. At the same time, she had no expectations that the conference would change anything for her. The decision was very similar to the choice to walk down certain streets on her daily commute to the university; they were simply there, in front of her, leading her to what she was going to do for the day and for the foreseeable future.

The new curiosity leaves her with a sour taste in her mouth.

Instead of exploring her capacities, her ingenuity, she is stuck fighting with herself. Instead of actively creating, she is suffering through dreams. It galls her to no end that the sole object of her curiosity is what she is hiding from herself.

Yet the thought that the mechanical woman will not be at the theatre tomorrow fills her with dread. Going through the event with just her creations, the steady, predictable rhythm of the crowd and the repetition of a blend of old and new lies would feel desperately empty. It would be like someone cut a large chunk out of her, temporary filled that part of her with an extra-ordinary instrument and then removed it, leaving nothing in its place.

She closes her eyes, breathes deeply and lets the sensations do what they will. Then she focuses on the new lies in front of her. Whole or empty, she still has a role to play.

Chapter 11

Rose, Etienne and Cesarine are sitting around the table in the backroom. Rose is looking through newspapers, Etienne is fact checking declarations he heard in the most recent session and Cesarine is vaguely looking towards the television.

"The local reviews aren't very kind," Rose points out to Cesarine.

Cesarine doesn't react. She contemplates the convex glass and the distorted world behind it as if looking through an eyeball into a monochrome brain. Even with the rules of order meticulously followed, the scene seems to slide towards entropy, pull itself back at the last minute and then slide anew. There is certainly an abyss just off-screen; a point of no return that delegates use to threaten each other, yet no one in the end is willing to be the reason the whole enterprise falls apart.

"I didn't think you read the local press," Etienne says.

"I was curious. It was mainly locals there; I counted maybe five delegates, and the whole place was pretty packed. So, one can assume that there would be a reaction in the city-level papers."

"They weren't locals, for the most part."

"No, you're right. I keep forgetting that locals in this town are a myth. Maybe 'long-timers' is a better term. In any case, not from the conference."

"The crowd seemed enthusiastic and really engaged. I thought that the questions would never end, and Cesarine handled everything really well. I guess I shouldn't be surprised; she has, after all, 'hosted one or two screenings before'."

Etienne looks over at Cesarine, who acknowledges his compliment with a slight smile. Her own abyss has taken center stage. She saw the mechanical woman in a hundred shadowy outlines during the screenings, without being able to convince herself that any of them was her idol. Every one followed the expected rhythm without fail; she alone could not stop herself from slipping.

"I know, right? These reviews aren't for the people who were there. If I didn't know any better, I'd say that they are for all the delegates who skipped it, but still need to have something halfway intelligent in their pocket to say just in case somebody asks them about it.

"Listen to this:

"The technical mastery of Vatsulka's animation is reminiscent of the feats of steel construction near the end of the nineteenth century. The world fairs of the time featured monsters of engineering that were both hideous and alluring. They were skeletons that hinted at life but lacked anima in themselves. Many of these techniques were later fleshed out to become buildings where people lived and worked. They became organs in the entity that was the modern city.

"As an anthropological exercise, the films still hold some interest. As anything more, they have little of substance to offer. One of the many occupations of people in these buildings is to create art that breathes, that fully engages us. A surfeit of these creations is all around us; there is far more out there than we can possibly enjoy in one lifetime. In light of this, there are far better ways to spend one's time than to watch Vatsulka's work.

"It has been argued that these films are comparable to a far-better-known monster: the Eiffel Tower. They may over time become beloved as symbols of a culture, they may become beacons for tourists from around the world. This is unlikely. The tower is a symbol left in context; it would be nothing without the city that pulsates around it. While the animation does have a place in the technical evolution of the art, it has none of the broad symbolism, support or appeal to become more than a historical footnote.

"Wow."

Rose and Etienne look at Cesarine, expecting a reaction.

The only consolation is that much of her dread had slipped over the edge, leaving numbness in its place. Cesarine is able to find her way from this stupor to her carefully structured functional indifference and asks, "Who wrote it?"

"Raoul P.," Rose reads out.

Cesarine nods with increasing energy. She actually finds the review to be perfectly reasonable, if somewhat flowery in its language. In her current state, reasonable is somewhat refreshing.

"It is best not to pay much attention to reviews," she finally says, keeping to the script. While she can openly agree to an article that calls her selfish, she cannot do the same for one that says apparently negative things about her work.

"I can't imagine most delegates saying anything like that," Etienne says. "The imagery is too rich."

"That's what they get for using local talent," Cesarine suggests.

"Wait, you know who this Raoul is?" Rose asks.

"I've met him," Cesarine admits, and then questions whether such an admission is wise.

"During the event? I couldn't spot the reporters in the crowd, and none of them stuck around afterwards to ask any political questions. Did you have a chance to talk to one or two after all? Not that it matters, given what he wrote."

"No. If he is who I think he is, we crossed paths once before under unrelated circumstances."

"Ah." Rose shuffles through the newspapers in front of her. "How about Henry S.? Eugene I.? Jack D.?"

Cesarine nods.

"Small world. Was it under the same circumstances? Do they have anything against you? Could it be personal?"

Cesarine shakes her head, before correcting herself. "Yes to the circumstances, no for the rest."

"Do you know much about them?" Etienne asks.

"No. Though I got the impression that none of them were above adopting a convenient position for a job."

"So, it is likely the same people who were behind the Chaulieu article."

"Did we make a mistake?" Rose asks. "The Chaulieu article undermined Cesarine as a person, which I still maintain is pretty much expected for great artists, scientists and all the rest. Now we have a bunch of reviews that say that she is not a great artist. And, we didn't get the freedom of movement soundbite for the audience back home."

Cesarine pulls the newspapers towards her, contradicting her own advice to not pay attention to the reviews.

"It was disappointing," Etienne says. "I don't think we made a mistake, though. Even if we did, there is no point in dwelling on it. We can now say without much doubt that there is a character assassination campaign against Cesarine that probably won't go away anytime soon. If the opportunity presents itself, we can at least show a solid example of Cesarine's work being freely available – so long as there is no government interference. We can also show how she volunteered to host an event and answer questions without directly, which is to say financially, profiting from it. We are in a better position to counter the Chaulieu article and can dismiss the reviews as a difference in cultural taste. The reviewers are, after all, long-timers or locals."

"I wish Valery was here," Rose sighs. "Not that your ideas aren't good. It would just be better to know more about what his intentions were when he came up with the plan."

"I'm sure that it's just a bug. He'll be on his feet in no time."

"Yeah."

Cesarine turns her back on the world captured by the television to take in the chorus of artful cynicism in the reviews:

There is a story about the first time the brothers Lumière

showed their short film, *The Arrival of a Train at La Ciotat Station*. Apparently, the audience panicked; they thought that the train was real and was going to run into them. Modern audiences are understandably amused by the reaction, lacking the perspective that movies were once completely novel. They have lived their lives in a world where cinematic illusions are commonplace.

The trick to experiencing Vatsulka's animation is to recreate that innocence in oneself. It is necessary to pass through the rabbit hole or wardrobe. Even with childlike naiveté, though, we expect to be plunged into a marvelous, immersive world. Vatsulka succeeds for a moment in immersing us in what seems like a grand mechanical universe. We are taken in just as the audience of the *Arrival of a Train* was.

Then, just as that audience realized that there was no train, it dawns on us that there is no universe. Once the initial sensation wears off, we find ourselves in a factory; we are surrounded by machines whose movements are purposeful, repetitive and limited. They can be hypnotizing but are in no way marvelous. Vatsulka's work does a disservice to our innocence by promising a vibrant escape from the tedium of modern life, yet in the end even falling short of an industrial dystopia.

The animation is simply tedious. It is like watching *Arrival of a Train* looped. Sometimes the movement is reversed, sometimes the train is made of musical instruments or rocks. The effect, however, is the same, and, even in 1895, it only worked once.

This review is signed Jack D. Cesarine recalls that Lucien introduced her to the group as the Lumière sister, so she is not surprised to read the comparison. She finds the critique far less just than Raoul's, though, since it does not take into account the underlying innovation. She would compare the series of films shown during the event to a time-lapse of a factory over several decades. No less tedious for someone expecting Narnia or Wonderland, no doubt, but not reducible to the repetition of the same movement under slightly different veneers, either.

"Whatever my ideas happen to be," Etienne is saying, "the most significant lesson is that it is far too easy to get sucked into this. We really need to stay focused on the conference itself."

"You're right," Rose replies. "The next topic is minorities. We did up some backgrounders at the embassy so all the areas will be on the same page."

Rose pulls a thick file out of her bag, leafs through it and finds packages to give to Etienne and Cesarine. Cesarine accepts it distractedly, still occupied with her chorus and not yet ready to move on to the next scene.

Rose continues, mainly for Cesarine's benefit, "Then we can move on to priorities and strategies, which are obviously not in the packages."

The selection of Cesarine Vatsulka's animation shown at the retrospective left me perplexed. At first, I thought that I was looking at a sort of abstract propaganda from the East, in the same vein as films that proudly show technical advancements in manufacturing or medicine. The intent of these films is to demonstrate how the East, with its centrally planned markets and research, is at least on par, if not more advanced, than the West. They have always left me with a sense of melancholy; people are denied the most advanced treatments and appliances because of a stubborn pride in a system that is far from ideal.

Don't get me wrong, it is not as if Western governments and corporations are perfect in making sure that people have the best quality of life. It is just that, when the Western system fails, the result is embarrassment and excuses. The shortcomings aren't typically used for propaganda.

In the program, it indicates that a substantial number of the films were made in the West, after the artist defected. I can only speculate as to the reasons for the lack of evolution in the work. The stripped-down mechanical worlds are perhaps a monomania, which is, I think, not uncommon among artists. That, however, does not explain the invariable presentation of the subject. Perhaps she was indoctrinated early on, in the same way as the filmmakers responsible for the straight-forward propaganda mentioned above. This does not jive with her position as a pioneer in stop-motion animation.

Then I think of Soviet Realism; ideological movies that ostensibly portray real life. For all the criticism that can be thrown at them, they cannot be considered mere propaganda. Beyond that, there is a sense of community, of struggle, of triumph and defeat; there is human drama. Vatsulka was not connected to the social currents of the East when she still lived there. In a sense, her work from that era was necessarily reflective of some aspects of her society. The essential aspects for it to transcend mere propaganda were nonetheless missing.

The disconnect obviously continued after she moved to the West. My sadness when watching Eastern propaganda is due in part to the artificial, yet no less real, barriers that deprive people of a higher quality of life. Vatsulka's animation gives me a feeling of frustration; there are no barriers in the way for that work to be developed into something more. I want to shake the artist, force her eyes open and compel her to experience the world right in front of her. Until her eyes are open and she is able to express more, I would recommend giving her films a pass.

"Do we have to do anything more than ensure that 'culture' is in the minority article?" Etienne asks.

"The biggest challenge is going to be defining what sort of minorities we are talking about," Rose replies. "We couldn't even agree on that at the embassy. Then, there are the problems of proselytism and the differentiation of rights in public versus private settings. The use of minority languages in official settings, such as courts, is all sorts of fun all by itself."

Cesarine takes a moment to absorb the substance of the review. She welcomes the critique that her work is not really at the level of art, even if she is not convinced that much of Soviet Realism could be considered art. Pragmatically, there wasn't enough passion in the mix for that. On the other hand, the idea that her work was a demonstration of the sad state of technical development in the East is idiotic; the supposition is a demonstration that the author knows nothing about stop-motion animation and does not care to learn.

None of that really matters though, since the main thrust is inadvertently all too accurate. Cesarine figures that it is only a matter of time until a relapse; her emptiness is tugging at her consciousness and her curiosity is whispering in her ear that she should really jump over the edge, just to see what happens. She wants to shake herself in frustration, to yell at her imagination to stop screwing with her.

Since all that seems to her insane and, even worse, pointless, she belatedly looks through the minority backgrounder. Rose's points about the difficulties of defining minorities and public versus private rights become quickly evident. Theoretically, the puppetry people of her old country would have a strong case for minority status, given how out of step they are with the rest of society. Their culture is built around public performance, though, so she can imagine how quickly the accusations of trying to convert people would start raining down. Even if puppetry was recognized as a nation or religion, it could only be practiced among the faithful. If it was recognized, however, perhaps other people would appreciate why the puppeteers have kept themselves separate from the activist artistic community that seems to include everyone else.

Thinking through the books she has read, Cesarine realises that none of them address the minorities of a country. Many of them touch on the difficulties of small countries neighboring large, belligerent ones, but that is a different issue.

"I agree; this is a complicated issue," Cesarine says in lieu of really contributing. "I don't know if it is because my old country was small or if it was something else, but minorities were never a concern."

"There was significant migration as certain regions industrialized, and during the war, so it was probably difficult to keep a cohesive community together," Rose suggests.

"And in your new country?" Etienne asks.

"I haven't been in contact with the local diaspora," Cesarine responds. "Maybe if I lived in the capital, the situation would be different."

Chapter 12

Cesarine feels that her inner dialogue has been compromised, so finds Lucien at his usual perch above the central hall. She suggests that they take a walk along the lake to take their minds off the conference. Lucien, seemingly in the middle of putting together another article, immediately abandons it and enthusiastically accepts the offer. They head down the boulevard in silence, as if busy organizing their mental houses for a guest.

"It was a good crowd at the theatre the other day," Lucien says, as the two stroll along the water.

"You went with your friends?" Cesarine asks.

"Yes, and I also read their reviews."

"What did you think – of the reviews I mean?"

"You want me to critique a bunch of reviews?"

"You didn't write one."

"I'm not sure why that should come as any surprise."

"It doesn't, of course. Then again, you could use the money."

"Despite popular belief – a belief I carefully nurture, by the way – some of my conference articles are accepted. I can, occasionally, thumb my nose at the news agencies. Phaedra is doing well, too."

"Thanks to some review driven controversy?"

"Just as the game is played. I wouldn't think that you would care, to be honest. You strike me as someone that does their own thing and doesn't care about much else."

"Did you meet the people who paid for the reviews?"

"It doesn't typically work that way. The group is well enough known now that outlets approach us with a subject, an angle and a word limit. We don't bother getting involved with the negotiations between outlets and managers, publicists or whoever else happens to have a finger in the pie.

"It was clearly connected to the other article – the one that suddenly appeared a short time ago – and, ultimately, to the conference. Probably the delegation from your old country, angry that you are here and wanting to discredit you. If it was me, I would have gone the other way; had they paid for a set of glowing reviews, the rumor that you and your delegation set it up would be running rampant right now.

"Unrelatedly, I recently read about mechanical trees with birds and frogs, among other marvelous inventions, in the throne room of the Byzantine emperor, Constantine VII, back in the tenth century. Apparently, at the time, that sort of thing was pretty common all over the Middle East, all the way out to India. In the chronicles of European visitors, they described it as magic, demons or witchcraft. It was kind of pompous and demeaning.

"That was not my intention when I called you Sorceress. But then, it's not as if I came up with the name. I don't know if the people who did come up with it meant that you were a godless heathen sprung from the deepest pit of hell or whether it was a compliment on how advanced your work really was."

"I never paid much attention. It didn't matter; the label still twisted expectations and added baggage. Despite your argument from the other day, if people come to the theatre expecting demons and witchcraft, they will likely see it, especially when they don't fully understand what is in front of them."

"I think it would be wonderful if you recreated mechanical birds and frogs and all that."

"What happened to doing my own thing?"

"Recreate them in your own way, of course."

"Right, sure."

"Only..."

"Only?"

"It would bring the mechanics to the surface; sort of like a coming of age, an opening of a chrysalis."

"Wouldn't that take the magic out of it? We aren't in the Middle Ages anymore."

"People will see what they want to see."

"Now you are making sense."

"Or, they will see a fantastic panoply of metallic songbirds, each one hinting at its ancestry with a splash of color here, a shape of a bill there. Then they open their beaks and let loose hauntingly familiar calls, only arranged in a way impossible in nature. Instead, it would be a grand orchestration that pushes the magnificence of the court into the realm of the divine."

"You don't imagine them flying around the throne room?"

"I don't think the ones from the Middle Ages left their tree, but that is just the starting point."

"It seems to me that you should create the world in poetry first. If I gave the birds a voice, you would be liable to lose yours. It would be a shame for that to happen before you were able to express it."

"See, I'd wager that you are saying that just because you think that I should do the work."

"It is your idea."

"That's true."

"What I don't understand is how you can take losing your voice so cavalierly. I know that it would terrify me."

"Wait, you still have a voice?"

"Of course."

"Because I didn't see any new work at the event. I mean, maybe you are doing research, gathering ideas; there are all sorts of possibilities. I just don't get that impression."

"I am not as prolific as I once was, but that does not mean that the flame has gone out. Is that why you pitched the Babylon idea?"

"Byzantine. No, it was something I had never heard of before that seemed really interesting. As for worrying about my voice, that sort of question makes me think that you didn't pay attention to the book I gave you. Which is fine, you didn't ask for it; you are under no obligation to read it."

"You quoted something about fear. I don't quite recall what, though."

"Crossing a bare common, in snow puddles, at twilight, under a clouded sky, without having in my thoughts any occurrence of special good fortune, I have enjoyed a perfect exhilaration. I am glad to the brink of fear."

"Glad to the brink of fear."

"I am aware that I don't live up to this. Coralie says that my goldfish-like attention span is not exactly conducive for much of anything. Still, experiencing even the most mundane things passionately is frightening.

"Am I scared of losing my voice? Yes. And, so long as my words are swept away during a moment of unadulterated exhilaration – as has been the case when I have seen your work – that fear is wonderful.

"I have pretty much resigned myself to the fact that I will likely never have experiences like Emerson did. I have some difficulty in seeing the poetry in a bare common. Even after a couple of collections of poetry out in the world, it was only with your films that I finally felt the experience of poetry. I constantly struggle with it; how can there be poetry without expression? Not having the experience though, using fear as an excuse to avoid passion; I can't imagine anything worse."

The conversation lapses into a silence marked by the incongruous rhythms of the waves in the lake and the steps of people and dogs on the gravel path around its edge.

"Now that I think of it," Lucien says, "Jack mentioned running into a woman in the editor's office of the newspaper he wrote his review for. He said that she was like you, only more together, focused and articulate. His words, not mine. He was there for something else, but got the job for the review immediately afterwards. That would be a twist: your long-lost evil twin is behind the nefarious plot to discredit you and have your life's work swept into the garbage bin of history.

"But, wait! She is as much in the dark as you are. She has been manipulated since her childhood in the state orphanage to do the government's dastardly deeds. She is a mere tool, her humanity smothered under a lifetime of indoctrination. Will her dear sister be able to reawaken her humanity before all is lost? Join us next week, when we find out if the world really believes that dear sister's art is actually a steaming pile of prosaic propaganda. And then they cut to a commercial for an amazing, magical and innovative household cleaning product."

"It sounds like you have it all worked out."

"Not so much. Due to network meddling, the scripts are constantly being reworked. That is why the series is so inconsistent."

"Ah."

"Sorry, we were talking about fear."

"Yes, we were."

"I don't imagine that you have that problem."

"Why do you say that?"

"You just do your thing, always have. Less now, perhaps, but still..."

"Maybe my evil twin sister fills me with fear?"

"Do you really care if you are discredited and have to quit the delegation? Does it matter if your films are not held up as examples of the highest level of achievement in the stop-motion animation medium for generations to come?"

"No, but perhaps your series should focus more on the personal, human side. The twin sister realizes that she is not alone in the world when she recognizes that a part of her is missing and that it is this stranger that she has been ordered to assassinate – at least in the sense of character assassination – who has or is that part. It would have to be mutual though, they both need to cross paths one day, look each other in the eye and share both the emptiness and the possibility that, together, they can be made whole.

"Now, let's say that dear sister is Emerson; she is in tune with nature, she passionately experiences everything around her. Evil sister is emotionally stunted from isolation and calloused from years of interactions with a hostile world. The story might have a happy ending, but until then, it would be torture for dear sister. She keenly feels the hole, practically a chasm, inside her. She can see the piece that would make her whole – probably more vividly when she closes her eyes, in her dreams – yet it is always out of reach. Her frustration turns to terror as it dawns on her that she may very well live the rest of her life incomplete, and that, in that state, her experience of snow puddles will never be what it once was."

"If evil sister knew about this weakness, she could, no; I don't want to go there. See, I had something light-hearted going, and then you had to go and turn it all dark and depressing."

"Sorry. I guess all I am trying to say is that there are different types of fear. I completely agree that the exhilaration-fear from the quote is worth being experienced and that it would be a shame to turn away from it. It is not as if we should avoid relationships and the like because we fear that we might lose the person we love. But that doesn't seem to be the whole picture."

Cesarine pauses before continuing.

"You are right; I generally just do what I do, though perhaps a bit less of late. Theorizing about emotions and nature and everything else is not a strong suit. I don't really know what I am talking about."

"But you have felt this other sort of fear?"

"Yeah, but that is probably the price to pay for a career of pulling the insides out of things and replacing them with whatever seems appropriate at the time. Out of habit, my subconscious likely took a piece out of me – not an essential organ or anything; I won't die from it anytime soon – tossed it and then realized that nothing fit in its place. Now it is panicking, which gives the rest of me a strong feeling of malaise. Nothing, in any case, like what Emerson was describing."

"So, no evil twin sister?"

"Maybe, but we shouldn't assume that I am the dear sister."

"Another twist; I like it!"

"I am apparently selfish and completely disconnected from my community and everything else around me."

"That can't be healthy."

"No one is really surprised when they find my dear sister tied up in my secret lair and discover that I have been feeding off her goodness for years."

"Who is out to discredit you, then?"

"I am. I have become increasing paranoid that my fame as an artist is making people too curious about my private life. I am obsessed with sinking back into obscurity, so I hatched this diabolical plan, which isn't really all that diabolical if I'm the one who's behind it. Anyway, the woman Jack saw was me, obviously not disguised well enough. I'll have to work on that."

"Okay, that's better; the darkness has passed. Sunny days are here again. Maybe you should animate that rather than the Byzantine court, give one of your films a narrative arc."

"I should probably just do the commercial for that household cleaning product you've been raving about."

"It would be more magical and, well, less Byzantine."

"Why does Coralie put up with you, again?"

"She uses me for my reviews, which is just as well. My last girlfriend tried using me for my wit, and that didn't go well at all."

"Seriously though, I can't imagine that sort of emptiness. Is that why you aren't making films these days?"

"I am less curious these days; as I've gotten older, doing my own thing has included considerably less doing. The fear, emptiness, is a mystery for me. Finding my twin sister is as good a theory as any."

"In reality, it's far too melodramatic and clichéd for my taste.

Still, it does spark my curiosity. I'll ask the group to keep an eye out for our mystery woman and Jack to pry some details out of his editor. We can all pretend to be investigative journalists for a while. It is the least they can do; there has been a steady stream of scotch since the reviews were published."

Chapter 13

On the days Valery doesn't have to be at the conference center, he has taken to staying in the room set up for him at the embassy, where the doctor who is part of the small military contingent can keep a closer eye on him. Rose is annoyed, as it means spending more time at the embassy than at the center, undermining her plan in setting up the backroom for greater efficiency. The shift pleases Cesarine, since the boxes containing possibly sensitive information had been moved to the embassy to join the unquestionably sensitive material already there, making the room quieter. It also proves useful for Etienne, who has started using the room for small out-of-session discussions with members of other delegations from the NATO crowd.

Cesarine is also content to spend less time in the center until the gossip dies down around her and her work. Despite the flowery language, Rose's prediction that the delegates would use the opinions from the reviews, as well as the Chaulieu article, as cover for missing the projection of her animation has come true. She can overhear enough in passing to recognize the recycled arguments. In other circumstances, she would be amused by how idiotic people sound, pretending that they are expressing well-thought-out, deeply held personal views. Instead, the whispers prolong the dread she felt since the day before the event. She had always considered the opposite of public effervescence to be apathy, but a good case can be made for public reprobation.

After the conversation with Lucien, she decided that, if she wanted to get over the lingering feelings of fear and emptiness, the best route was to focus on the 'woman' part of the mechanical woman. It is probable that she is a real person, even if the 'mechanical' proves to be a figment of Cesarine's unhinged imagination. The short walk to the embassy with Etienne and

Rose for their regular strategy meeting with Valery seems to her an opportune occasion to broach the subject.

"Do you remember the first area session I was at?" Cesarine asks Etienne. "The topic was freedom of expression, as I recall."

"Vaguely," Etienne replies. "I'd have to look at my notes for the details."

"There was a woman with my old country's delegation. She looked like me; average height, thin, dark hair, pale."

"Okay. She doesn't ring a bell, but my attention was focused on the table."

"I don't know if she was present at the sessions before then, but she wasn't there afterwards. I don't know why I am just making the connection now – I am not even sure that it is a connection – but I remember that she was staring at me for a while and then she left. After that, the Chaulieu article appeared. Is there a way to find out who she was?"

"Maybe. There are attendance records, though with the number of people that come in and out of the room during a given session they aren't always accurate. I can look though, and ask around."

"Thanks." She has more confidence in Etienne's abilities than she has in Lucien's friends playing at being investigative journalists.

Regardless of the gossip and the mechanical woman, the conference continues. Ten minutes later, Cesarine finds herself in Valery's room at the embassy with the rest of the team for the meeting. Valery, sprawled out on a settee, takes a moment to study his team. Then, as if sensing Rose's simmering irritation, decides that this is the right moment to say a few words about his condition.

"I want to let you know that there is nothing really wrong with me; you don't have to worry that I am going to shuffle off this mortal coil anytime soon."

"That is good to hear," Etienne says.

"So, what is the problem?" Rose asks.

"No one knows, the doctors can't find anything. I just have spells of weakness from time to time. In the last couple of weeks, they have become more frequent."

"When did they start?"

"Back in Africa, on a trip to Egypt, maybe seven years ago now."

"And you didn't think it worth mentioning then? What would have happened if you hadn't made it back from one of your jaunts in the old medina?"

"The people who needed to know knew. It was the main reason why a security detail was assigned to me. They were able to use the pretext of an uptick of violence in the country, kidnappings in the mountains, to justify it. That would be somewhat more difficult to do here."

"Why did they choose you to lead the third area?"

"I imagine because I was the best suited for it, the same reason that you are here. It is not as if our aptitudes were of much use where we were. As you have pointed out on a couple of occasions, superpower penis measuring did not generally require nuanced diplomacy."

"Not because the ministry thought that this area was useless, so having a delegate who might faint in the middle of a session would be embarrassing but not actually important?"

"Does it matter?"

"Of course it matters. If I've been shelved already, and because I followed you..."

"You haven't been put out to pasture. You, all three of you, are on the front line of the most important continental conference our country has ever been a part of. There is a lot of cynicism floating around; no matter how much we accomplish here – and we have already had a real influence on the content of the final document – there are people who persist in believing that small countries are necessarily powerless and that human and cultural rights are fluff.

"If you can't see this for the opportunity it is by now, I'm not sure that I can help you."

"It isn't just your condition... No offence intended, Cesarine."

"Did anything happen in Egypt?" Etienne asks, trying to redirect the conversation.

"Nothing that explains the spells. It was a small get-together to talk about cooperation in North Africa and, more broadly, the Mediterranean. The whole thing was awkward, since it was after the Six-Day War and the canal was closed. It was fairly obvious that Egypt wanted to portray itself as confident and in control, which was far from the truth at the time."

"Wasn't it the Egyptians who blockaded the canal?"

Cesarine sees that the military men in Etienne's head have laid out a map of the area and are contemplating it, scratching their chins.

"Yes."

"And yet they wanted to promote international cooperation?"

"It was a complicated time. Nothing came out of the meetings, of course. There was a lengthy discussion at the ministry beforehand on whether we should even go. There was a strong contingent that felt that the conflict between Israel and Egypt should be resolved before accepting any sort of invitation. The argument that we should maintain a minimal-yet-positive relationship just in case it might prove useful in the future won out.

"Strangely, our hosts invited us to take a trip to the canal. I understood that that had been the standard visit offered to foreign dignitaries since it opened a hundred years ago. Nobody had thought it through at the time. I suggested that we go to the residence of Ferdinand de Lesseps, the developer of the canal, instead. They agreed, so off we went."

"You didn't think of suggesting the pyramids, or something along those lines?"

"The pyramids don't have the right symbolism. They speak to past glories that do not resonate with modern Egypt. The canal shows that Egypt is at the center of modern international trade. Only, of course, at the time, with the canal blocked and Israel occupying the Sinai, it had a somewhat different message. On the other hand, Lesseps was a French diplomat, so my suggestion could have been taken badly. It wasn't, thankfully.

"Anyway, there was a huge sandstorm on the way to the town. It was over by the time we had arrived. When we got out of the vehicles, everything had a yellowish tinge; the sand had made its way into every nook and cranny."

"That sounds typical across the continent, if one is close to the desert," Rose observes.

"You're right. It was not my first storm, and it probably only seems huge in retrospect. That was the first time I felt weak. I had to lean on the car and pretend that I was just taking a moment to observe the house. I have had them off and on ever since. I occasionally wonder if it does have something to do with the sand, but that doesn't make much sense."

"So, as you said, no real explanation."

"No. And that is enough of that. You now know all there is to know. Please keep it to yourselves; the other areas do not know. Besides the change in venue for some of our meetings, every-thing should continue as normal."

"What if you have an episode during a session?" Etienne asks.

"It is just a moment of weakness; if I am sitting down in a session, it's not a problem. If I am walking in an open field with nothing to lean on or against, on the other hand..."

"Where are we with the minority article?"

Cesarine has lost interest in the minority question since the delegates across the areas decided to limit it to ethnic, religious and linguistic groups. Rose jumps into the topic, trying to make up for her earlier comment about being shelved. Etienne goes over the important connections and patterns from his notes, but it is difficult to say exactly how engaged he is, since the officers in his head still seem to be considering the situation in Egypt. Cesarine is somewhat envious, as her sense of Egypt's geography is woefully inaccurate. A map would be helpful, though she would quickly find the tromping of heavy boots irritating.

It then strikes her that everyone on the team is out of place in one way or another. Though she noticed the heavy coat Valery wrapped himself in when they met at the university and a series of throwaway phrases about Africa since, she hadn't bothered to put them together. It hadn't mattered; she had already decided on his wooden head, in line with all the other delegates at the table. He was a convenient hour marker, sitting in his habitual place at the table during sessions as the shadowy hands of the skylight frame passed over. The wooden head was not immediate though; she recalls being impressed with how quickly he had turned the department break room into a temporary office. The transformation and coat said far more about him than the solid, classical marionette-like brain. Yet only the latter stuck with her.

She had not asked about his previous assignments, any more than she broached the subject with Rose, Etienne or, really, anyone. No one in the team has been completely comfortable with their position as part of a delegation of a small country at a big conference, covering an area that has never gone very far at the international level. They are career diplomats, so far more at home here than she has been, but that does not say very much.

She feels for Valery at least insofar as his condition resembles her own; to be weakened by something so real yet so frustratingly elusive. Beyond that though, she knows that she is the person Chaulieu described in his article. She is forced to wonder what she hopes to accomplish in searching for the mechanical woman. Perhaps her idol had some characteristic that triggered her reaction, but there is no reason to think that the characteristic would be any less superficial than Etienne's previous assignment with NATO influencing what she saw in him.

Despite the physical differences that would at the very least make being identical twins impossible, the woman did have similarly dark hair, pale skin and a relatively slight build. Common characteristics for people from the old country. Still, that could have been enough for her to see the idealized version of herself. Then her imagination shorted out and her inner life became rather hellish. She used this stranger as an armature that she fleshed out and clothed to become the person who haunts her. Finding her would change nothing, just as the sandstorm altered nothing about what she sees when she looks at Valery.

The conversation has turned back to the interminable conflict of the public-versus-private expression of minority rights. Cesarine wonders if life would be better or simply more interesting if she did have a dear- versus evil-sister relationship with the mechanical woman. The train of thought is quickly derailed though by the question of whether Valery fears walking in an open field; if being deprived of control over his body leaves him with a similar frustrated anxiety to her own.

Chapter 14

"Can we introduce a new article?" Cesarine asks the team.

"We can bring it up," Valery replies. "If we can get general agreement, new wording can be introduced. It's better to not focus on whether it will be an article, a clause or just a couple of words inserted into something already in the document. If delegates agree to an idea, all the rest can be work out after. What do you have in mind?"

Cesarine hesitates before answering.

"Freedom from fear," she finally says weakly. This is the first original idea she has had since the beginning of the conference. It is not an original idea in a broad sense; since she has started thinking about it, she has noticed it in her readings and the world around her. It is, however, the first contribution she has thought of that comes primarily from her own experience, even if the experience has nothing to do with her life in the old country.

"That seems quite broad. Do you have anything specific in mind?"

Cesarine has a great deal she could say, none of it interesting to anyone, not even to herself. It would be worse than explaining the motivation and process behind her animation, where she can at least lose herself in generalities and abstractions. Of course, worse would actually be a relapse into a waking nightmare as time continues on around her; a catatonic silence as her team looks at her, expecting a response, finally having their suspicions of her mental instability confirmed. It is best, though, not to tempt fate by dwelling on that thought.

Instead, she puts the originality aside and focuses on the recycled, unwilling to approach the precipice.

"Fear was a basic tool to keep people in line and society running smoothly in the old country. There were all sorts of mechanisms that played into it while avoiding the pitfalls of rights and obligations caught in other articles. For instance, laws were created in such a way as to make everyone guilty. It has been illegal to possess my work since I left, for example, just as it has been for the work of everyone who has defected. As Chaulieu explained, it is improbable that many people have reels of my animation lying around, but almost everyone has books, music and movies available in more popular formats. Even if they get rid of them, the fact that they once owned them is still against the law.

"Everyone has something hanging over their head that can be used if they step out of line. A number of articles have a clause against arbitrary arrest and imprisonment, which this gets around by using a formal, apparently non-arbitrary law. People self-censor out of fear of going to jail for a record they owned fifteen years ago."

Cesarine's train of thought continues to a strange coincidence; her lack of fear when she was living in the old country puts her in the same boat as most of the protagonists she has come across in her reading. The fear was palpable around them, but they were either mostly indifferent to it or it was drowned out by pride, lust or patriotism. This indifference or insensibility was powerful enough that they were ultimately unmoved not only by the consequences of their actions on themselves but also on those around them. For dramatic effect she supposes that they had to be that way; otherwise they would have done nothing and would have never been at odds with the system. For some reason, her indifference has led her on a completely different path; one utterly devoid of conflict. Maybe in her next life, she will make a model protagonist.

"Should I continue?" she asks.

"I'm struggling with how to differentiate the abuse of law from what every state does, at least sometimes," Rose says. "I mean, state power comes in part from the threat of force. One could say that people who might otherwise murder or go through a red light don't out of fear of the consequences. Murder could be grounded on non-state principles but the rules of the road are arbitrary in a fundamental sense, even if they are predictable and formal, so not arbitrary in the sense that we use it here."

"I don't think that that is analogous to Cesarine's example, though," Etienne argues. "What she is saying is that people are arrested and tried because they said or did the wrong thing, but they are charged with having run a red light a long time ago. Only none of the traffic lights have a yellow light, ensuring that practically everybody runs a red light at one time or another."

"And it isn't just laws," Cesarine continues. "It covers admission standards for schools, membership rules for artist guilds and institutional employment..."

"Do you have any personal experience of this?" Rose asks.

Cesarine is taken aback by the question. She was proud of being able to use her work as part of the first example. She wants to ask why that isn't enough.

Sensing Cesarine's reluctance, Valery clarifies.

"When I was explaining my condition the other day, I said that nothing had changed. That is not entirely true. Since the beginning, when you were looking through the file boxes, certain members of the delegation thought that it was best to keep you in the background so as to not ruffle any feathers. It was my decision to have you come to sessions. With the gossip surrounding the article and the reviews, there is a push to bench you or even send you home permanently. Though my position has not formally changed, my influence on the chief delegate has lessened somewhat.

"It is nothing significant, and I hesitate in saying anything about it since my bringing it up may give the impression of a lack of cohesion in the group, which really isn't the case. Everyone has always had a variety of ideas and positions that frankly make the delegation stronger. It is far better than being in an echo chamber.

That said, anything you can offer that clearly ties to your unique experience is especially helpful now to make sure that you can stay on the front line.

"I understand that this is unfair to you; it is not your fault that I can't defend your position as well as I would prefer to the hierarchy. I apologize for that. That is, however, the reality of the situation, so anything that we can do to help make your position stronger would be greatly appreciated."

This reality influences Cesarine's view of the world in a way the characters of her teammates does not. It is likely, she imagines, because it directly affects her future. The reality is incomplete, though, particularly as she does not know who exactly is responsible for the rather successful campaign against her. That does not stop her mind from racing ahead and assuming that the mechanical woman – either as a construction of her imagination or her evil twin – is at the center of all the machinations. The plot would be especially diabolical if it forced her to approach her inner pit in order to save her job.

The plot doesn't hold together though, as she is not all that attached to the job. The more she thinks about it, the fewer differences she sees between the post-sandstorm world and the situation beforehand. The team has been pushing her to contribute more from the beginning, so, while she might be closer than ever to being sent home, she fails to see why she should change her course. She just hopes her imagination agrees.

"The reviews were overly dramatic and obviously paid for," she says, "so if they are influencing the chief delegate's take on what to do with me, it is probably best that I go now."

"And I was the one to suggest that you set up the event that made the reviews possible," Valery adds. "I am not saying that anything, especially how tenacious the rumors have been since the reviews, is reasonable. It's just a question of working with what we have and making as obvious as possible to everyone that you are a great asset."

"It would have been worse had we gone with my original idea of making the screening an official event," Rose says.

"We don't know what the reaction would have been."

"Didn't the minister want Cesarine included in the delegation from the outset?" Etienne asks.

"Yes, but his interest in that faded as he became less and less involved in the conference. If the chief delegate told him that the initiative was not working out, he wouldn't protest. Sometimes, independence from political engagement can be a double-edged sword."

Cesarine sits back, hoping that the back and forth continues and her freedom-from-fear idea is forgotten. In a group that requires context and nuance, original ideas are too much work. Unfortunately, the discussion ends quickly and the focus returns to her.

"Look," she says, "as I said before, in contrast with the reviews, the Chaulieu article is fairly accurate. I don't have the experiences you are looking for and your insistence that somehow, at the end of some cobweb-filled hallway of my mind, there is something more, is getting a bit tiring. It would actually make more sense to talk about Chaulieu than me. He stayed even after his books were banned and, as far as I know, he has family and is involved in the community. I don't know the details, but he must have been kicked out of the writers' guild and has to deal with making a living in some unrelated field. His books were thick, complicated tomes, and it seems like he has been reduced to putting out a meagre newsletter that a school newspaper would put to shame. And he has likely gone to jail, or at the very least been harassed, for it."

As she talks, her imagination decides once again to prove its independence. She finds herself stuck at a window of Etienne's military headquarters, looking in. The interior is bustling with activity, as if before a major offensive. She senses that the mechanical woman must be in there somewhere, but the confusion of fatigues and faces turned towards the map on the central table or buried in reports make it impossible to know for sure. As with the maddening vision of the theatre before the projection of her work, she is unable to move; even the map is a mystery to her.

"But you are just speculating, no?" Rose asks.

"Yes, of course. I tried reading one of his books once, but I couldn't finish it. I know that they were banned, but can't tell you why. I know that he decided to stay, but have no idea what his motivations were. I mean, it is obvious from the article that he values community solidarity, but only insofar as that does not compromise artistic creation. I suspect that his reasons for staying are about as incomprehensible to me as those for me leaving are for him."

Cesarine pauses to let the frustration drain from her voice and back into her dream, where it belongs. She focuses on Valery, whose solid-wood brain seems, at least for the moment, immune to her imagination's modifications. She is too scared to look at Rose, whose production-line inner workings would be very sensitive to interference, all the while knowing that she can't avert her eyes for long without appearing awkward and dysfunctional. Of course, staring with fascination at alterations only she can see – a fascination marked by irritation at what she is hiding from herself – is not exactly the model of functionality, either.

"There was no one from the School of Puppetry in a similar situation as Chaulieu?" Etienne asks. Cesarine hears aggressive tones in his voice that she has never heard before and is sure are illusory.

"Perhaps, but I wasn't aware of them." She struggles to keep her voice even.

"And no one among your family and friends?"

"No. I was never very close to people, though."

"What about your government contacts?" Rose asks. "Not in

the sense of being like Chaulieu, but rather in instilling fear in any way; threats, violence, innuendo..."

"They were all supportive, I suppose. The true believers were a bit overeager, the others, professionally distant. No one was really interested in the work, just in the fact that something creative yet not subversive was happening on their watch. The details weren't that important."

Cesarine knows that she is, once again, heading in the wrong direction. She should really pass off some of what she has read as her own experience. As the reviews noted though, stories are not her strong suit. That was the point of reading fiction; she still needs to put herself into a role, something more nuanced than artist, delegate or functional. She can't bring herself to go that far. Still, she can't stop with so little on the table.

"That was the point, though: there was a great deal of positive reinforcement; of encouragement for bettering oneself, at least superficially. My animation was a neutral model that others could follow. It was not pro-government, which would have been a negative thing had it been created at the end of the fervent forties – it was still considered with ambivalence by the most idealistic – but fit well with the normalization of its time. At some point, someone figured out that it was easier to control a society of unengaged people who were willing go through the motions at appropriate moments than one where everyone held deep political beliefs.

"It is the only explanation I have for the official popularity of fairly abstract work that should by all rights have had a very limited audience."

"Once again," Rose says, "I am under the impression that we could be talking about almost any country. Next you are going to be talking about bread and circuses, or cake and consumerism."

Cesarine is confused by this, thinking for a moment that Rose is comparing her films to popular distraction, which is absurd. Then she thinks that the comparison is being made between her work and insubstantial filler, which makes more sense; mere propaganda for the virtues of superficiality, the hypnotic repetition of a mechanical existence. She is not quite sure, so she gives a possibly related tautology a try.

"Fear does tend to work better when people have something to lose."

She is about to launch into Lucien's Gandhi argument when Valery speaks up.

"I think that the initial point might be getting lost. As helpful as it would be in the larger context to have your experience, personal and professional, support the idea of freedom from fear – although, in a way, I am happy that it doesn't – we shouldn't reduce the idea by trying to shoehorn it into a role for which it is ill-suited. We would be sacrificing our goals for this conference to rumors and petty squabbles, which, frankly, should be below us.

"Separating it out, freedom from fear is very important, be it the fear of being beaten by roving militias for wearing certain clothing or of being fired from a job for having different opinions than those of one's managers. Rose's argument, that fear can exist in any country, strengthens the idea, while also putting it in a better position for it to be accepted by all the delegates. So, so long as Cesarine is okay with it, let's leave her fate to the side and figure out how the idea can work. If we're lucky, the rest will sort itself out."

Cesarine nods, content that she can look at Valery without awkwardness and ignore whatever tricks her imagination may be trying to play on her.

"I like it," Rose says. "If we can get text stating that no one should live in fear, with some obligations tied to it, that would be a big win."

"It is a very broad idea; well beyond the scope of the third area," Etienne points out. "I would say that the first step is to get the other areas of our delegation on board."

Chapter 15

It turns out that the mechanical woman is not that difficult to find. Either that or Lucien's friends actually proved to be competent investigators, which Cesarine continues to doubt. Jack's editor had a contact at the embassy who knew immediately who she was from the description. It turns out that the editor never did catch her name, so his contact provided him with her first name, Violet, the only name he seemed to know. From what he said, it was clear that she was a fixer who worked for the central committee of the government. She was no longer in town, but she might come back if the message was adequately enticing.

Her role as a floater was confirmed by Etienne; nobody in his diplomatic circles had a precise idea of what she did, but those with a history of bilateral relations with Cesarine's old country tended to cross her path at one time or another. Most of Etienne's contacts were unable to help, but he chalked that up to the relatively minor role the old country had played in international politics, particularly after the invasion.

Cesarine asked Lucien to have a message sent simply saying that she would like to meet her. A reply suggesting a one on one, giving a time and a place a couple of days hence, arrived without delay. The location was a café close enough to the center to be convenient, while being far enough away and on a peaceful-enough side street so there would be little chance that other delegates would see them. Given the incessant rumor mill of the center that still hadn't completely gotten over the reviews, Cesarine appreciated the choice.

As soon as she accepted, her anxiety fell away, her imagination was at peace. It was strange: so much could go wrong; the woman could be an insipid bureaucrat, a marionette devoid of the inner workings necessary for spontaneous thought, a camera who, once she had recorded Cesarine's presence, was pulled from the event before her faulty construction betrayed her, before a limb fell off in midsession, hitting the floor with the chaotic noise of a bag of loose parts. Cesarine's imagination did not take the relay, though, and the momentum of this line of thinking was lost.

She then tried to entice her imagination with Lucien's long-lost-sister theory. Maybe there was a well-hidden connection that gave her the assurance that they would be able to fluidly communicate from the beginning, as if they had known each other all their lives. Her imagination stayed inert, seemingly uninterested in anything she came up with. It was as if her decreasing enthusiasm over the years had just reached its nadir, yet without despair or misery. It just was what it was.

The day of her meeting, Lucien is still trying to convince her that he should come along, just to be sure. He continues to burn with curiosity to meet the person who has had such an inexplicable influence on his sorceress, even if he is careful not to use the name in her presence. In the end, he accepts just telling her how to get there – she can't miss it, with the small Catholic church directly across the street – and a promise that she recounts all the interesting parts, with a particular focus on any exposition of her sister's nefarious plan.

When Cesarine arrives, Violet waves at her. She is sitting at an interior table in the mostly empty room, halfway back and facing the street, busily scribbling notes on some documents among the papers spread out in front of her in neat piles. It is like meeting Valery all over again, in an impromptu office that is formalized by the presence of such a strong personality. The only difference is that Violet's papers appear far better organized. As with Valery, Cesarine has to force herself to focus on the person in front of her and imagine the inner workings. Her imagination gives her a blank wall, as if one of the innumerable upgrades of the original rusty bikes parts was armor against her gaze.

By the time she reaches the table, the papers are gone; put

with remarkable efficiency into a thin bag that seems far too small to hold them. When she sits down, the sole server approaches the table. She orders a green tea, Violet, another coffee. Then they sit in silence for a moment before Violet speaks, in the language of the old country.

"I like this café because of the church across the street. It is where members of the Polish delegation sneak off to, when they have the opportunity. They are all of course officially atheist, but that's just politics. Seeing them here gives a sense that life is larger than what can be captured at the conference and in treaties. It's refreshing."

Cesarine is not sure how to respond to this, so she assumes the worst.

"Do you write down their names so you can use it against them later?"

Violet laughs. "That would be absurd. It has to be one of the worst-kept secrets of the Polish diplomatic corps. The government actually promotes it, so they have a convenient excuse to reassign staff as need be.

"I have to say that I am amused that you responded to a comment about how refreshing it is to see people do things beyond the political sphere by reducing my supposed motivations to politics."

"Do you like my work?"

"Yes, though I confess to prefer films with a stronger narrative voice."

"Insofar as you like my animation, then, do you like it in a non-political way?"

"Ah. I suspect that you are perfectly aware that the government used your work for political ends, at least before your defection. I would say that I appreciate it in both ways."

"Though you have been appreciating it in a more political way of late?"

"Speaking of reactions; the inclusion of defectors in delegations has been first and foremost a provocation. Your case is perhaps the most blatant, since you spent so much time in your workshop back in the day that you missed everything that was going on around you. Are you surprised that there has been a response?"

"No, I suppose not."

"I think that you surprised everyone by joining the delegation. It was clear why they asked you – it's not as if there were many options in such a small country – but you have never been one to get involved in these sorts of adventures. If you don't mind my asking, why did you say yes?"

Cesarine still does not have a good answer to this question.

"I guess I was spending less and less time in the workshop and needed something else to fill the days."

"Teaching was not satisfying?"

Cesarine shrugs. Sometimes it was far more satisfying than what she is doing now. It is not something she wants to get into with Violet.

"So, besides paying hack reporters to write negative reviews and distribute old articles, what do you do with your time?"

"I help things run smoothly. It's a vague description, I know, but it would be difficult to be more precise. I am a fan of music, particularly the piano – in a completely apolitical manner, I might add. The films that I prefer among your work are those that use musical instruments as the inner workings for inanimate objects. The piano, even a grand piano with the lid open and the soundboard visible for the audience to see, has always struck me as a closed instrument. You freed the action, the feeling of the hammer striking a string, for the audience while leaving it in the confined, intimate space of the ordinary objects that surround us.

"How did you set up the action, was it always animation?"

"It depended on the piece. Most of my work has actually been a mix of animation and live motion, even if the focus has always been on the former."

"So you filmed real pianos?"

"Not exactly. As you said, they were cramped and difficult to work with. There were all sorts of broken-down pianos floating around in the capital, so I just took what I needed. The sound was added afterwards with a functioning instrument, which was a challenge in itself, at least at the beginning, since pianos are hard to mic, especially on a non-existent budget and without a studio. That is one of the reasons why I preferred string instruments."

"So you had the same technique, whether it was live action or animation?"

"With animation, the mechanism had to be tightened and the string replaced with a wire or the equivalent so they wouldn't move between shots. One time, I just drew lines that approximated the vibration on transparent foil and cycled them between shots. The technique depends on what I wanted to accomplish."

"The wire was special?"

"No, not at all. You can get it at any hardware store. I use the same stuff for my Introduction to Armatures class. Armatures are essentially skeletons; the basic ones are just wire and wood, with maybe some cardboard on the bottom of the feet to pin them down. One of the difficulties in the beginning was having wire thick enough to show up on screen. It was the opposite of today, when even very thin wires are visible and distracting."

Cesarine puts herself on autopilot to answer the questions, as she would at a screening. Violet stays on the technical side, which makes the discussion pleasant enough. She feels though as if she is treading water; there is no frustration or fear, but there are no answers. The woman in front of her is agreeable, and obviously intelligent and well-versed in both Cesarine's background and the machinations of diplomacy. She could very well be the mechanical woman, the ideal that Cesarine had always dreamed of for herself. There is, however, no way of knowing. There are after all no hinges visible and she has, as far as Cesarine is concerned, already passed the Turing test.

That is all well and good; it is not as if she really expected to be having coffee with a machine, although she still on a certain level wishes that she was. The problem is that she can still feel the emptiness inside her and now she has no idea what to do with it. Reaching out to Violet was of course worth it, if only to know who this stranger really was. She knows enough now to call it a day, even if she can continue to talk about the technical aspects of her work all day long. That is the one positive thing she can mention to Lucien when he badgers her later; Violet's questions do not wander into philosophy, art, magic, or any domain that she finds disagreeable.

"It's funny," Violet is saying. "Most people like talking about themselves, at least when they get going. While you do seem to enjoy talking about your work, if I didn't know any better, I would say that your thoughts were elsewhere. I suppose that I am being impolite; you were the one who asked to meet, so what do you want to talk about?"

Cesarine is once more at a loss. "I just wanted to meet the person behind the article and reviews. I hadn't really thought through what would happen after that. I don't suppose there is any point in asking what you plan on doing next?"

"We haven't decided. The idea behind the article and reviews was to make a point, nothing more. In a way, it is better for us if you stay on as a delegate, since you are relatively harmless and a distraction to the rest of the group. On the other hand, a scandal that forces you out could destabilize the delegation. In any case, it is not a high priority. I think, going forward, that little effort will be put into it, but we will take advantage of opportunities as they come up."

"You are quite nonchalant about doing things that could ruin people's lives."

"I have my moments. Anyway, as I said earlier, it is the price of playing the game. In your case, it is, I will be the first to admit, strange, as I can't figure out what you have to gain by being here.

There is really no upside to it. All the other defectors were dissidents or in conflict with the government in one way or another. They were well-connected in their communities and cared deeply about them. Participating in the conference is another way to help that community and, for some, to assuage their guilt for abandoning their compatriots. Of course, there is also one in particular who just misses being at the center of attention, but his motivation is no less clear.

"When I looked into your background, I hit a blank wall before long. Sure, there was – maybe still is – a great deal of curiosity regarding technique and mechanics that showed up in your file at the National School of Puppetry and has given direction to your work ever since. Your output has slowed significantly of late, which could indicate a drop in curiosity; you might have finished exploring the areas you wanted to explore and no longer have any goals to work toward. I would ask you but it is evident that you don't know yourself, any more than you know where you want to take this discussion.

"What I don't know is what is behind the wall – if anything is. There are no hinges, openings or anything that would be available in one of your films. There could be a sophisticated logic back there that puts my paltry calculations – calculations that can be summed as 'see an opportunity', then 'react within certain parameters' – to shame. Perhaps it is the mental equivalent of a piano, or a far more sophisticated instrument that is well above ordinary interests. While my focus is on the ground, looking for base motivations for your defection and your presence here, there could be a poetic explanation staring me in the face.

"But then you only play at being an artist to meet other people's expectations, so why would anything poetic be behind the wall? It has been somewhat frustrating; one of the reasons why I am good at what I do is that I get an accurate sense of who people are rather quickly. You are definitely the exception."

Cesarine's thoughts stay fixed in one spot, stunned by Violet's analysis. She suddenly remembers the tea in front of her, tepid and over-steeped. She takes her time pulling the bag out and putting on the saucer, and then taking a sip.

"It is safe to assume that there is nothing behind the wall," she finally manages. "Thank you for meeting with me."

Then she walks out without looking back, her mind, with the notable exception of her imagination, in turmoil.

Chapter 16

Valery asks Cesarine to stay behind after the group strategy meeting in his room at the embassy. Once Rose and Etienne have left the room, he explains that the chief delegate wanted to have a word with them and that he is as much in the dark about the subject as she is. They wait in silence until, a moment later, the door opens and a man with the workings of a steam locomotive enters. His quick, over-energetic movements as he joins Valery and Cesarine in the seating area give the impression that his regulator and safety valves are malfunctioning and so has too much built-up pressure. Cesarine suspects that her imagination has given her this snippet more out of habit than out of an active desire to create. In any case, she is surprised that he is so different from the wooden countenance of other senior delegates.

Despite the fact that they have never been formally introduced to one another, the chief jumps right in to the matter at hand. It is as if he can only suppress the impulse to move for a short time, or risk explosion.

"An unfortunate incident regarding Ms. Vaculka was brought to my attention yesterday. I hope that we can establish the facts quickly so we can deal with the situation in a timely manner and go back to concentrating on what we are actually here to accomplish at this conference."

He looks at Valery and Cesarine in turn, waiting for a sign from each that they are on the same page before moving on.

"Ms. Vaculka, did you meet with a foreign agent this past Wednesday at the Café Courtois?"

Cesarine does not respond, unable to connect Violet with the notion of foreign agent.

"A woman by the name of Violet?" the chief prompts.

"Yes."

"Valery, were you aware of this meeting?"

Valery, taken by surprise, guesses that this has something to do with the article and reviews. Etienne had mentioned in passing that Cesarine had asked him to look into a person she thought was responsible.

"I knew that Cesarine and other members of my team were looking into the people responsible for certain documents released recently that have undermined the delegation, yes."

"Did you know about this specific meeting?"

"I ask my staff to use their discretion when informing me of their work. Cesarine did not feel that I needed to know about this meeting, likely because nothing came out of it."

"Ms. Vaculka?"

"That is correct," Cesarine responds, though it had never occurred to her to tell Valery about the meeting, regardless of the outcome. The answers she was seeking were personal, even if there was some overlap with the delegation's work. "While I was able to confirm that it was Violet, on behalf of the government of my old country, who had the Chaulieu article distributed and the negative reviews on my work written, I was not able to find out any more. Since we had already concluded that all that was the work of my former country, I did not see the point in informing the team."

"Have you participated in team strategy meetings?"

"I have been present at the meetings, yes."

"So, you are aware of both the area and overall delegation strategies for the conference?"

"Yes, I am aware of them."

"Have you received any training on how to approach foreign agents, particularly those who represent conflicting interests with our own?"

"No, I have not yet had that opportunity."

"Valery, would you have let her go to this meeting unsupervised had you known of it?"

"It depends on the specifics, such as whether the agent would have been willing to meet with more people, whether the language barrier would have been a problem..."

"Let me rephrase: in general, would you let an untrained member of your team go to a meeting with an agent of a non-friendly country without supervision or support?"

"It would not be my first choice."

"Would doing so be against protocol?"

"Yes."

"Well, at least we agree on that. Ms. Vaculka, did you share delegation strategies with Violet?"

"No."

"Why should we believe you, when you purposefully kept the meeting a secret?"

"As I said, the meeting was not important; nothing came out of it."

"Perhaps we could give you some leeway if the meeting was with a delegate at the conference, or even a member of the local embassy staff. Violet is a high-level agent who appears to have come into town for the meeting. We have since lost track of her. It is of no use to try to convince us that it was insignificant; people like Violet do not accept to meet with someone without good reason."

"Can I ask how you heard of it?" Valery asks.

"A member of the Polish delegation inadvertently mentioned it."

"That was not inadvertent," Cesarine says. "Violet chose the café because Polish delegates went to the church across the street. She said something along the lines of liking to see delegates doing things that went beyond politics, that it made them seem more human. But it was just so we would be seen together."

"Are you saying that it was a setup?"

"It looks that way."

"Who asked for the meeting?"

"I did."

"How?"

"Through one of the journalists responsible for the negative reviews. He spoke to his editor, who arranged it through a contact at the embassy."

"And you knew this journalist before the review was written?"

"I met all four of the journalists who wrote the reviews beforehand. The team is aware of this."

Valery nods in response to the chief's questioning glance.

"Were you coerced into asking for the meeting?" the chief continues.

"I would not say coerced, no. I was provoked. Since I joined the delegation and showed my face at sessions, someone has been trying to tear me down both personally and professionally."

"One of the reasons that several people thought it best that you stay in the background." The chief gives Valery a hard look.

"Attending sessions has been invaluable for learning how a conference like this works. As you alluded to earlier, it is not as if I have had formal training or experience in diplomacy. Without the sessions, I would have had very little to contribute to the team."

"What have you contributed, exactly?"

"Right of residence, to balance out freedom of movement. Freedom from fear, which we are still working on."

"Cesarine has been involved in research, writing discussion papers and clarifying strategy across the board," Valery adds. "Given how little experience she had coming in, everyone on the team is impressed with how far she has come."

"Ms. Vaculka was asked to join the team because of her intimate knowledge with the systems and policies of her old country, as well as those of other small, Eastern states. None of the contributions made seem to take advantage of this knowledge. In fact, although you have not had the time to be educated on how to deal with non-friendly foreign agents, I understand that you have not only socialized with local reporters but also familiarized yourself with the writings of real dissidents from small, Eastern countries. It is knowledge that can be picked up at the corner bookstore that you have been using as the basis of your contributions, largely because you were never involved in the dissident community."

"That does not change the fact that the contributions are real," Valery says. "Cesarine has been a unique asset, regardless of whether that comes from her artistic background, her lack of familiarity with the dictums of diplomacy or because she was a leading figure in the protests that preceded the invasion. We need to look at this practically."

"That is a very good idea, Valery. Practically speaking, Ms. Vaculka has committed treason by communicating, without lawful authority, secrets to a foreign agent that favors a foreign power. That is the reasonable interpretation of the facts, regardless of what Ms. Vaculka may suggest her intentions were. What's worse, she has shown a marked disregard for the consequences of her actions. Anyone who can't see the peril of sneaking off to meet with someone like Violet is dangerous to the whole delegation, whether their intention is to divulge secrets or not.

"Add to that socializing with reporters who subsequently damage the efficacy of the delegation to continue in its core mission and lacking the knowledge to fulfill the role that the minister envisioned in the beginning, and I fail to see any practical reason not to send her home."

The chief pauses to let his diatribe sink in, looking back and forth between Valery and Cesarine, daring them to say something. Both stay silent. He then addresses Cesarine.

"The upshot of this is: thank you for your efforts but we no longer have any use for your services. Valery will work out the details."

With that, he rapidly stands, nods to Cesarine and Valery, and then heads to the door with so much pent-up energy that it seems like he is going to crash through it. He stops at the last minute to open the door, looks back to see that neither of them have moved and then is intercepted by a delegate for a quick hallway meeting. The force leaves the room with him; both Cesarine and Valery feel drained from the encounter.

"You aren't having a spell of weakness right now?" Cesarine asks.

"No, no. I'm fine. How are you doing?"

Cesarine shrugs.

"The chief doesn't realize that you don't think like a diplomat; that the lines between who it is appropriate to talk to and who one should avoid are blurred, if they exist at all. That doesn't matter, though, since everything associated with the conference is inescapably political. Honestly, if I knew as much about you at the beginning as I do now, I'm not sure that I would have offered you a place in the delegation. This is not a negative thing, as far as I am concerned; being here has just put you in an impossible position. On one hand, you are supposed to have all these non-conformist, dissident qualities – that still must fit into a certain mold of political non-conformity – and on the other, you are required to get up to speed on diplomatic norms in a shorter time than most career diplomats have to learn the ropes. Maybe other countries have a process for this sort of thing, but we don't. And we certainly don't have a metric to rein-in unrealistic expectations.

"Are you sure that you are all right?"

"Although I did not expect this exact end to the adventure, I knew from my days of sorting boxes that my time here would not last long."

"Ha! Yeah, Rose was pretty angry about that. I hope that you take more from the adventure than the presentiment of impending failure. Not that diplomacy, and particularly long, drawn-out conferences like this one, is known for its excitement, but I hope that you have gotten something positive from the experience. I do expect to be a major character in your next film."

Cesarine smiles weakly, wondering if Valery or any of the others would recognize her versions of them.

"You remind me of a fellow I became friends with in North Africa; Robert," Valery continues. "His family lived there for a couple of generations, up until the war of independence. At that point, everyone came back to Europe to avoid the violence and political upheaval, but he decided to stay. No one knows exactly why; he didn't really fit in to the local culture, but then it would have been unlikely that he would have done any better anywhere else. His family, especially his sister Esther, when she was alive, has worried about him ever since. He doesn't typically answer the phone or respond to mail, so the family got into the habit of contacting the embassy. That led to a couple of visits a year for me to his place in the old medina. He isn't a talkative sort, but has always been welcoming and pleasant. He just has – how do I put this – different priorities. He does his own thing, though I have never been sure what that is.

"In any case, he isn't a well-known artist like you. Perhaps the comparison is too much of a stretch. Only, you both have a talent for being within cultures, being connected to others, and yet being somehow aloof from them. He was in the middle of the maelstrom of war, witnessed the creation of a new country, yet was absent, in his own world. You witnessed the fall of democracy and the rise of an idealized socialism, then the crushing of those burgeoning ideals under the treads of invading tanks and the creation of a formal, kind of bourgeois, socialism, and yet you were absent – in your workshop until all hours of the night, as you mentioned. Yet your work – and Robert's as well, I have no doubt – is still somehow important for the government and for the society overall.

"The point to all this rambling is that I think that we are all better off with people like you and Robert doing your thing and not being forced to follow the rules of this place. I also think that Léon Chaulieu was very short-sighted in saying that your choices have been selfish. We need people who are able to follow an independent path, who can avoid getting caught up in the maelstrom, just as much as we need dissidents and others who are engaged in the day-to-day politics of their community.

"And, you are sure that you are doing okay?"

"I suppose that I should go and pack."

"Do it tomorrow; take some time to wander around the city, away from the embassy and the center. There's no rush."

Chapter 17

"It's the Vonnegut paradox," Lucien observes.

"Here we were," Raoul says, "hoping to give you a send-off with the scotch we bought at your expense and Lucien has to go and ruin it with his flights of fancy."

"The more important issue is that he is wrong," Jack adds. "If the paradox is what I'm thinking he's thinking of."

The attention of the group focuses on Lucien.

"Well, okay, it's the *Slaughterhouse-Five* paradox, to be more precise."

"I knew it! That means that you are wrong, by the way."

"How am I wrong?"

"The paradox is necessary, not voluntary."

"Why don't you explain what you are talking about?" Coralie asks.

"That would be helpful," Henry says.

"Fine," Lucien says. "Our hero, and likely Vonnegut himself – the book was fairly autobiographical, I understand – witnessed the firebombing of Dresden. Only, the sole reason why he lived to tell the tale was because he was being held in this famous slaughterhouse, which protected him from the bombs. So, while he was in Dresden at the time of the bombing, he did not really witness it. The paradox being that the only way one can be a witness to certain events is to be present but not actually a witness."

"Cesarine's case is completely different, though," Jack argues. "Vonnegut, Pilgrim or whoever else would be dead had they really experienced the firebombing. Cesarine could have gone out, been part of the protests, and even seen the tanks roll into town, without dying. There were almost no casualties. The other guy's case – Robert, right? – might have been comparable; I understand that the fighting was intense in the medina during the war of independence. For Cesarine, I don't buy it."

"It's not so much that she might have died – I certainly concede that the two cases are dissimilar in that way – but rather that she would not have been able to create works that have become iconic of that time and place. There was simply no way to do both; she could have either participated in the events or she could have made her films."

"Don't you love how they talk as if you aren't here?" Coralie asks Cesarine.

"I tend to focus on the rhythms of their voices and ignore the content. A trick I learned when not participating in the culture of my old country."

"Makes sense. Kind of like muzak, except less soothing."

"It is not encouraging us to buy things or be more productive, that's for sure."

"I have to agree with Jack," Henry says. "Look at the other celebrity delegates; it's mainly a group of famous writers and scientists who also found the time to be politically active. Stop-motion animation is time intensive, sure, but so are experimental physics and the writing of a detailed fictional account of the events leading up to the creation of the Soviet Union."

"So, you plan to go back to the university?" Coralie asks.

"Yes, when the next semester starts," Cesarine replies.

"I am astonished that you are taking this so calmly. I would fight, make noise, something. I also wouldn't be so forgiving to this lot for having written those reviews."

"I guess that I don't see it as something worth fighting for."

"What do you consider worth fighting for?"

"I don't know, at this point. There is something to be said for the peaceful existence I had before coming here."

"Just don't turn into Lucien."

"Hey!" Lucien cries. "What's wrong with me?"

"What's wrong with you, my dear, is that you have chosen a profession – a profession that can be wonderful, rewarding, important, and all the rest for the right person – simply because it would take too much time and effort to do what you really want – and have, somewhere inside, the talent – to do."

"Well, my lovely little carbuncle, it seems to me that you are forgetting the abject poverty that came with such pursuits. My poetry could have been a success by now, but I would certainly be dead. I may be romantic, but not so much as to wish for my own untimely end, even if, by some miracle, my passing was a veritable chez-d'oeuvre of somber beauty.

"Yours would have been picture perfect, of course, but then you've had practice with that sort of thing. I'm sure that I would have gotten distracted at the last minute and messed everything up. At least with my articles, the bad taste in one's mouth left by the first one's awkward phrasing and insincere gravitas is washed away by the acerbity of the next one. And, bonus; we can eat!"

"See?" Coralie says to Cesarine. "Don't be like that."

"There is little chance."

"Good."

"I don't think we heard the story of your meeting with Violet," Jack observes. "You only talked about what happened afterwards. Is she the puppet master you suspected she was?"

"She reminded me more of a chess master who was playing against multiple opponents at the same time. She handily won the match against my delegation – or against me, but I got the impression that I was nothing more than a target of opportunity. The minister had the temerity to put a symbol of shame for her country front and center at an important conference. She then thoroughly undermined that symbol and set things up so the delegation did the dirty work of getting rid of it. The chief delegate essentially believed that I was a disgrace for the delegation by the end.

"She was curious about me, undoubtedly because I am somewhat different than the diplomats and dissidents she usually comes across, but it was an academic curiosity that she didn't put much into. The moment I walked into the café, she knew that the game was over. Her mind was already partially occupied by her next move on a board likely half a world away."

"What exactly was she curious about?" Lucien asks.

"The same thing as you, I imagine. She had already done a pretty exhaustive analysis on me, but seemed to think that she was missing something, that there must be something more to such a well-known artist, sorceress or whatever else people choose to see. It was disconcerting, how accurate her take on me was, even if she didn't realize it.

"I was the same way, though, building up unrealistic expectations beforehand. No, actually, I was worse. I imagined the impossible; that she was the perfect mechanical woman, the archetype of what I have always tried to create in my animation, or – I blame Lucien for this one – my evil, but not necessary profoundly evil, twin sister. At least it was conceivable, if highly unlikely, that I could have been Emerson or Méliès.

"In the end, she could have been anything. The chief was absolutely right; she was a highly trained foreign agent who let me see what she wanted me to see. One of my teammates – former teammates – would be sorely disappointed to hear me say that; he would say that I didn't spend enough time observing the subject and too much on my sketch..."

"I like that far better than the overwrought firebomb paradox," Eugene says. "Cesarine has spent so much of her life in her workshop that she has forgotten to look outside from time to time."

"That seems too 'stop and smell the roses' for me," Raoul counters.

"That works really well, actually," Jack says. "Instead of stopping to smell the flowers, she is busy making flowers, mechanical flowers that nobody has ever experienced before. She plants the flowers and everyone else stops to smell them. Some think that they are a miracle of nature, others that they are black magic, and so on. They ultimately become entrenched in the culture, maybe even a symbol of it. But then, just when the powers that be have trumpeted to the world that they are a great nation because of this wonderful achievement, the flowers start popping up elsewhere. This, of course, brings them great shame and they sic—"

"A group of underachieving journalists on the creator," Coralie interrupts, "who write scathing reviews of the flowers, saying that they are neither wonderful nor magical, but rather examples mediocre propaganda. And, lo and behold, people throughout the land, too preoccupied to smell the flowers themselves but sufficiently motivated to glance at the reviews – just so that they have something to say around the water cooler, you understand – take the opinions expressed as gospel. The flowers, as bright and colorful as they have always been, fade from people's minds and end up trampled underfoot."

"... I was going to say the dark creation that sprang from the same seed; the mechanical woman, etc., etc., but I like your version better."

"But really, it wasn't the world, it was only the people from the conference," Henry points out. "The screening was very well attended. I don't know if those who were there found the flowers bright and colorful, but I am sure that they couldn't have cared less about what we thought."

"Violet really knew her audience," Raoul remarks.

"The question I have," Lucien says, "is whether all this navel-gazing, this lack of observation, this obsession with the interior, can be anywhere near as fulfilling and, well, passionate as our interactions with the world?"

"Okay, that's just too serious," Jack replies. "Can't you just regale us with tales of the demonic mechanical creations of Babylon?"

"Byzantium."

"Wherever."

"Wait," Henry says, "does the interior bit have to do with the people at the conference or Cesarine?"

"Someone is hooked. Now, we are all lost," Jack cries.

"Cesarine; the creation of such magnificent mechanical flowers without the exhilaration of experiencing a field of violets in the Italian countryside. The flowers having, of course, no relation to our dear foreign agent."

"If I had an Emerson-like connection to nature," Cesarine responds, "I suspect that I would be missing a great deal by not being more observant. But, then, who among us has been truly euphoric about a snow puddle?"

"Isn't 'snow puddle' an oxymoron?" Raoul asks.

"Regardless of where you get your inspiration," Coralie interjects, "I think we all hope that your stay in our little town has been on the whole a wonderful experience, despite what some of us here have done. We look forward to seeing your new work, once you have gotten away from what I understand is a very tedious affair."

"Hear, hear," the chorus shouts.

The conversation shifts to future plays and articles, giving Cesarine a sense of what life is going to be like once she is gone. She realizes that the repartee is a form of public – or, at least, communal – effervescence. She is moved by it, but not profoundly or passionately. It is more of a pulpy yarn than the bustle of a well-designed agora. The discussion, particularly when it swirled around Violet and the mechanical flowers, has reinforced her suspicion that no amount of effervescence in the world around her will have much of an influence, no matter how much she might wish that it could shore up her flagging curiosity. So long as she is not condemned to the self-imposed misery associated with the mechanical woman, she doesn't find this conclusion overly troubling.

She is the first to leave, explaining to the group that she has to get up early in the morning to finish packing. Lucien accompanies her to the door.

"We will see each other soon, I have no doubt," Lucien says.

"Why is that?"

"You aren't going far, and I don't think I will have much trouble convincing the others that your next screening is a perfect excuse for a road trip."

Cesarine reflects for a moment on how easy such a trip would be for them, and then arrives at a strange idea, at least for her.

"Are you still in contact with the reporter who told you that everyone called me the Sorceress in the old country?"

"I haven't seen him in a while. Why?"

"I was just wondering how difficult it would be to have my films smuggled back there."

"In more popular, more compact formats? To address the criticism of the Chaulieu article?"

"It was just a passing idea. If my run-ins with Violet are any indication, I should really avoid thinking that way."

"Perhaps. Do you want me to look into it anyway?"

"Okay."

Chapter 18

Cesarine gazes at her shadowy ceiling. She waits for the alarm to go off, knowing full well that it won't. She has had no reason to set it, not yet having classes to teach, administrative meetings to attend or anything else of that nature. She should do something, be active in some way, but she figures that her experience at the conference should suffice as the major accomplishment for her hybrid government service leave slash sabbatical. The paperwork was rushed in order for her to be free for the start of the conference, so most of the details were left vague and approximate. She was under the impression that the university was more than happy to have one of its academics at a conference that Valery had described in the most glowing terms. The potential for recognition was just too good to pass up, particularly after the disappointingly low profile Cesarine had kept since joining the faculty.

Today, though, is somewhat different. She does have to get up at some point and head along the indifferent streets to the university for a meeting with the leadership team of the School of Marionettes. The meeting is late enough to justify not setting the alarm, however, in retrospect, she wishes that she had done so anyway, if only to play out the routine from before the conference. On the other hand, the memory of the conference host's voice that whispers to her is certainly more pleasant than the combative ideologues on the radio, sparring with talking points dulled from overuse.

She certainly doesn't want to hear anything about the conference. The form of the host's voice is adequately separated from its content, but the same cannot be said for those that hammer the same note without nuance or subtlety. It ends up being a distraction from the peaceful, uneventful existence she has fallen back into.

This pleasant cocoon extends along the streets that lead her to the university, only faltering in the face of the nervous energy of the students. The semester is coming to a close; the presentation of term projects is immanent. Cesarine is nonetheless content that the meeting is happening now, before the grading is over and the energy becomes loud and boisterous. The calm returns when she enters the waiting area of the dean's office, though she feels exposed without the comforting envelope.

When she is ushered into the office itself, she is met by the dean, the vice-dean academic and a person she has not met before. The dean, Cyril, is the only person she has ever imagined as a piano. He is also fairly unique in that his inner workings travel through his entire body. If he lies down on his back, his piano-like nature becomes clear; with the white keys blending into his hair, the action around where his mouth is and the strings, after the pinch point at the neck, extending to his extremities. His range is limited to an octave and he looks somewhat unbalanced with three black keys on the right and only two on the left. The entire back of his body is a soundboard, hinged appropriately for human-like movement. In contrast to Violet's assertion that even a fully open lid of a grand piano leaves its insides seeming cramped, Cyril's insides seem to protrude from his frame when his lid is up, giving a musically inclined observer the desire to take a bow or pick to the strings in order to enjoy a uniquely hybrid sound.

She completely forgot about Cyril when she was talking pianos with Violet, not that remembering would have made a difference. She is not inclined to talk about what she sees in people, for obvious reasons. Perhaps she should have said that behind her blank wall was a psychosis characterized by regular visual and auditory hallucinations and the delusional belief that Violet was the ideal mechanical woman, the mechanical woman she had always wanted to be. Then she would beg her to show her how to take off her own head and open the hatch under her left ear. She would confess that her one dream – her lifelong obsession – was to be able to observe the clockwork in her own brain. Violet would have undoubtedly humored her and followed through on her plan to have her fired for treason – or maybe would have planted something so she would have been arrested and sent away; she was obviously a ticking time bomb.

Rachel, the vice-dean, has precisely machined armatures in her head, busy blinking her eyelids, pulling a chain to move an arm, observing a multimodal vital-signs monitor and a hundred other tasks. The light shines off their shiny metallic forms as they move about smoothly and quietly, their joints fitting perfectly together. Cesarine always feels a touch of jealousy, as her own armatures are never without flaws.

"Hello, Cesarine. Thank you for coming in," Cyril says as Cesarine sits at the small meeting table on the opposite side of the room from the desk. "You know Rachel already, of course, and this is David, from H.R."

Cesarine nods to David, who is busy writing on a pad of paper, and then waits for Cyril to continue. While her imagination continues the already established visions for Cyril and Rachel, it is unresponsive to new people, at least those without the overwhelming presence and energy of the chief delegate. After the fear and frustration that it generated during the conference, Cesarine is just as happy that it does nothing now.

"As you know, the university is in a delicate position; it aims to be a space of open discussion and inquiry of even the most unpopular ideas, but it also relies on significant government and donor support to function. We understand that you were let go from your position as delegate at an international conference for treason. Treason is a term that has a lot of baggage; it is not as if you were trying to start a war or assassinate a head of state. Even so, it is rather serious and could compromise the ability of the university to fulfill its mission.

"Essentially, although your role here at the school is not in itself sensitive – the last time I checked, there weren't many state secrets mixed in with the marionettes – you are a member of the university community. You represent, to a certain extent at least, the institution. In many ways, you have been an exemplary representative over the years. You are certainly one of our best teachers. I am sorry to say that that does not mean very much compared to a charge of treason. So, for the sake of continued funding and overall institutional harmony, we are going to have to let you go.

"It's funny; we were talking before you came in about the history of the treason-and-espionage clause in the standard university employment agreement. Apparently, it was put in place for scientists, to ensure that the military wouldn't have a reason to go elsewhere with its contracts. This is the very first time it has been used.

"I don't know why I bothered saying that. It can't be of interest to you at a moment like this. Anyway, from here on out, you will have to be escorted everywhere you go on university grounds. Rachel will take you to your office, though, if I recall correctly, there is not much there.

"Does anyone have anything to add?"

Everyone, including David – who apparently wrote down everything the dean said – shakes their heads.

"Okay. Cesarine, please give me your keys to the school."

Cesarine pulls the keys off the ring and puts them on the table. Rachel then leads her out of the room. She follows, lacking the will to do anything else. She feels disoriented, unsure of how to function under the circumstances. Since her return, she had the impression of being in a different world, a world that had only a tenuous connection to the conference. Excepting her inoperative imagination, she thought that she could re-enter her old life without repercussions. Losing her job so suddenly deprives her of the central point of reference from the old life, leaving her with a numb indifference.

Once they reach Cesarine's office, Rachel asks her to sit down. She obeys without thinking.

"Well, that was an unfortunate scene," Rachel says. "Unfortunate, but necessary."

She waits for Cesarine to react, then, when it becomes clear that Cesarine's face is going to stay as absent and empty as her office, she continues.

"The whole episode smells rotten, like a witch hunt. You were certainly never convicted of anything. How do we know what really happened at the conference? Why should we trust a bunch of bureaucrats we don't know who could have all sorts of motivations for pushing you out?"

She waits again for a reaction, perhaps for Cesarine's side of the story, but nothing happens.

"There is, of course, a practical reason for the university pushing us to fire you, but that certainly doesn't make it right. Cyril and I discussed it, and we came up with a plan. It isn't ideal, but, well, it won't hurt to hear it. I would understand, though, if you would prefer having nothing more to do with us.

"You can't stay on as a member of the faculty, and can't teach. On the other hand, as you know, we rent out studio space fairly regularly. It benefits the students to rub shoulders with working artists, we have always thought. I think that we can manage to rent your studio to you for, say, a dollar. It would include access to the usual equipment and materials, of course. So long as you keep it quiet – word of mouth only, no advertising – you could also tutor to make some money.

"Look, it isn't much. I know that you haven't been exactly prolific with your animation since you've been here; maybe you have to find a teaching job elsewhere to make ends meet. We will do what we can if that's the case; you'll always have a good recommendation from us. Do think about the offer, though."

Rachel gets up to leave.

"Don't I have to be escorted on university property?"

Cesarine asks.

"People from the university rarely step foot in the school, so I don't think we have to worry about that. And, as Cyril said, it is not as if there are any state secrets around here. Oh, and Anne has a set of keys for you, if you want your space."

Cesarine is left alone in her office, though she supposes that it is no longer really her office. It is just an empty room with cold cinderblock walls. She does appreciate the offer, at least insofar as it proves that her relations here are not so fragile as to completely collapse from her mistakes at the conference. The offer only makes sense, however, if she can function creatively. She tries to imagine something, anything, on the desk in front of her. When that fails, she tries to imagine a door in its surface and some sort of activity below. Nothing.

She concludes that it might be just as well that her creativity has left her. She has, after all, become quite talented at faking being an artist, among a variety of roles, in order to meet other people's expectations. According to those like Lucien, the very fact that she did not experience nature, in the pragmatic sense of having a fully realized encounter with the world around her, means that her ability to make art should have been fatally compromised from the beginning. Yet, the very same people still take her animation to be art.

She hadn't been very successful at being a delegate, but, as Valery pointed out, it's not as if she was given much time to learn the ropes. One of the upsides of having lived a life of functional indifference is that she hasn't had the motivation to do much of anything that costs money. So, she has time to figure things out; she can accept the offer for the time being, while looking for teaching gigs at her leisure. This fits the only significant motivation that she does feel at the moment, which is the curiosity to see if she can pull off creating without creativity.

Chapter 19

Returning home after working out the logistics of the new arrangement with Anna, Cesarine finds a letter from Lucien:

My Dear Lumière Sister,

I am sitting on my usual couch on the terrace overlooking the turbulent sea of delegates. They still snub the food, and, each day, I die a little more inside, watching it be taken away after breaks, so nobly stoic in the face of its ignoble fate. Yes, since you ask, I am supposed to be writing an article right now. The group has just started discussing monitoring and standing committees, which, in retrospect, makes the debates on the substantive articles seem like pure entertainment. Still, the article will be written, not to worry.

There was actually a substantive article; no, scratch that, it's not an article, nor a clause; the group hasn't decided where to put it yet, so it is really just a floating phrase; discussed recently that you might find amusing. It is not exactly a phrase either, but I digress. 'Freedom from fear.' Now, okay, I am not so blinded by my own take on the world to think that the expression is not reasonable in certain ways. Living in daily fear of repression, violence, etc. is not exactly anybody's dream. I can always point to it when Coralie needles me about the endless detour from my poetic path and say, "Look! It's an internationally recognized right to not live in daily fear of dying in the gutter!" If it works for my interests, how can it be bad?

I also admit that there is a difference between 'freedom' and 'obligation'. If people get off on feeling fear, then all the power to them, the final clause could say. But for those who want to live a peaceful existence filled with warmth and security, well, that's okay too. Fear is not a requirement for a good life, it could add, in case the reader hadn't yet caught the gist of it.

Even if it is not an obligation, however, including an expression like this puts fear squarely on the wrong side of the tracks. It sets normal as a life without fear, or at least a life that minimizes fear. To my way of thinking, that is terrible; it encourages living in a bubble, avoiding new experiences and sensations. There would be no passion!

Am I being hypocritical? Coralie would say that I am being a hypocrite. There is probably some nuanced position, arrived at after a thorough examination of the taxonomy of fear, that would avoid such contradictions. There are probably a dizzying number of treatises on the subject. We even talked about it, in the evil-sister days. Fear is, I would say, an intriguing topic of study.

As nice as nuance is, it does not translate well into treaties and conventions. Of course, when they do put in some nuance, like in the minority rights article, they usually screw things up, so it is probably better that they don't try. I mean, whose bright idea was it to limit minority rights to ethnic, religious and linguistic minorities? What about cultural or gender minorities, to just name two? As an aside, my article on that topic was accepted.

It's even worse with freedom from fear, though, because the group has no clue what to do with it. They need to include it somewhere, so they will probably just plop it in some clause or other that isn't completely unrelated.

I said at the beginning of this rant that it might interest you, but you probably just want to leave the whole conference debacle behind you. That's what I would do, but then I am not exactly reputed for my steady nature. The boys and I are still keeping a lookout for your femme fatale (I have unanimously decided that she is not related to you, after all), just in case she comes back around to stir up more trouble, but it doesn't seem like she's been around. It doesn't help that we are all going off Jack's description of her, a description that borders on outright caricature. We don't expect her to have horns, for instance, though we don't want to completely rule it out, either.

Even if you have decided to not block the conference out of your memory, you were never all that enamored with Emerson, I think. Passion, (constructive) fear, the intimate experience of the world around us; none of that is at the base of what you do. You are all about the mechanical flowers. So, forgive my rant if it is of no interest; it actually wasn't the point of this letter. It just amuses me that fear is going to make its way into the final document.

The first point of the letter is to let you know that I had a wonderful chat with a reporter from your old country over one or two too many drinks. It was not the same guy as before, which leads me to wonder, with my statistically significant sample of two; are all the journalists from your old country that fond of alcohol? Anyway, we got to talking about the still-well-known Sorceress. You have slipped from being famous, I am afraid to say. Interestingly, he had read the Chaulieu article for the first time at the conference and had already had the idea of smuggling copies of your work in better formats into the country.

He dismissed it, though, since most of the older generation had seen your animation before it was banned and most of the younger generation didn't care. I did ask why he believed that the younger generation didn't care, to which he replied that, due to widespread censorship, they were cut off from older works and didn't see any connection to themselves. I thought that this explanation was marvelous, since it implied that your animation was well-imbedded in the culture, even if you yourself didn't have much to do with it.

Suffice to say that he rethought his position when I told him that the Sorceress was a friend of mine. He wouldn't be interested in your old work, but, if we can get him Betamax and VHS tapes of new animation, he would be willing to smuggle them in. I guess that the market is pretty well split between the two formats and he was not sure which one would go over better. He hoped it would be Beta, since it is the smaller of the two, but he would have to see after a first run.

I don't imagine that this is helpful, since you haven't made any films in a while. Still, the option is there, at least until the end of the conference, if you do create something new. I, of course, would still like to see a recreation of a Byzantine court, but I suspect that those interested in your work from the old country would be looking for something different.

The second point, which overlaps with the first, is that Clive, the manager of the cinema where your films were screened when you were here, reached out to me. Apparently, word has gotten around that I am the best person to talk to if one wants to contact you. I am starting to feel like your agent, which is bizarre since agents need to be at least somewhat grounded. Given the success of the event from his perspective, he would be more than happy to set something up in the future if, once again, you have new work. It looks like Henry was right; the reviews had no real impact on the world outside the conference.

For my part, I would obviously like to see new work; to have my words dissolve in the overwhelming exhilaration of a new experience, even if much of what I would feel is undoubtedly due to my overly sensitive nature. There is no use trying to force it, though, and a fear-free existence of teaching at a school in some sleepy provincial town certainly has its attraction. In any case, let me know if you want to do something more; if, perchance, you do notice a glimmer of magic in the world around you.

That's all I had to say. Now to go find a snow puddle to be afraid of. And then, an exciting article on the proposed makeup of the standing committee that is supposed to monitor the implementation of whatever the final document turns out to be.

Lucien

Cesarine is amused at Lucien's reaction to 'freedom from fear'. She wonders what he would say if he knew that the expression was arguably her most important contribution to the conference. At least he already knows that they are not of the same opinion regarding Emerson. The rest is probably just a matter of degrees. Thankfully, Lucien does not have to rely on the conference text to get a sense of her position, any more than the audience of the screening had to rely on the reviews to appreciate her animation.

The more substantive part of the letter is very useful for her. The most significant challenge of maintaining the functional side of functional indifference is not knowing the expectations of the role. She struggled with that throughout her time at the conference and, without the frame of being on the university faculty, she was not sure how to proceed. In the beginning of her career, satisfying her curiosity was enough of a direction. The rather superficial curiosity about whether she can create at all does not act as much of a guide, and that is all she has at the moment. The letter gives her two audiences to produce for, with specific expectations attached to both. She cannot guarantee that she can come close to meeting those expectations – in the end, it is often best to deviate from them quite substantially – they nonetheless offer her some much needed direction.

At the same time, she decides to send a quick note to Etienne to ensure that the options are legitimate. She is naïve, but not so naïve as to blindly follow Lucien's suggestions.

Chapter 20

Cesarine quickly finds her new rhythm, largely because much of it is based on her old university schedule. The arguments on the radio have returned to their status of meaningless sounds on the same level as the old announcement reminding people that shoes could be bought at the shoe store. The route to the school remains the same, with its comforting lack of effervescence. Her first task in what the school calls her studio, but what she prefers to refer to as her workshop, is to clean and organize it. She has rarely stepped foot in it over the years, doing maybe one small project a year to practice new techniques and familiarize herself with new equipment that she would be using in her classes the following academic year. Once she had viewed the results, she had the habit of throwing away the reels, just so they wouldn't wander. She had not been motivated by the knowledge that she was under-mining her future as a recognized artist by not releasing something into the world on a regular basis.

She has decided that another small animation would be the best way to start now. After, she will aim to create something both more important and more in line with what one might consider a natural evolution of her work. The deadline for the important project is before the end of the conference, which, given the pace of negotiations, gives her plenty of time.

The first animation is a pared-down yet more-active version of Lucien's Byzantine court fantasy. Cesarine mixes in some of the ideas from the mechanical flower conversation, aiming for a mechanical construction that is unabashedly metallic, bright and colorful. She starts with a throne room that hints at cosmopolitan riches, as a royal court at the intersection of Europe and Asia would be, without being overburdened by ornate detail. The room is filled with courtiers and foreign dignitaries, who are mere clothed armatures with very limited movement. The vast majority are fixed in place and can only nod, shake and turn their heads in response to the activity of the emperor. The emperor, stuck on his throne, can gesticulate freely with his upper body and can open his mouth. One dignitary is on his knees in front of the emperor as the scene begins, reaching out to offer him a present.

The present is a fruit. The emperor makes the dignitary wait in that awkward position as he proclaims a variety of things that the audience cannot hear clearly. The court nods and shakes its many heads in unison. Then, the emperor deigns to take the fruit, but just holds it as he continues his discourse. The dignitary lowers his arms but rests on his knees, apparently waiting until the emperor takes a bite. After a moment, the emperor considers the fruit in his hand, and then throws it into the audience. The dignitary is startled upright, though still on his knees, and all heads turn to watch the fruit's flight. A couple of courtiers in its path have sufficient movement to lean forward or backward, so it misses everyone and lands on the tiled floor.

When the camera swivels back, we see that the dignitary is now standing with the others. The discourse continues, as does the nodding and shaking of heads. The dignitary misses his cues though and the emperor starts gesturing menacingly in his direction. Then there is a loud crack at the back of the room. All the heads, along with the camera, swivel to see that the tile has cracked where the fruit has landed. The emperor is suddenly silent and the room watches as the tile continues to break apart under pressure from the fruit that has sprouted. The roots and stem glint momentarily in the light, until the tile disintegrates completely and the fruit falls under the floor.

One of the courtiers who were able to bend out of the way of the flying fruit cautiously bends forward to look down the hole, before jerking upright. A moment later, a seedling grows out of the hole. It is made out of banded metal of different colors that spiral to the top, where they split to form single-colored branches that sprout simple, oblong leaves as the court looks on. The only sound is that of the roots continuing to burrow under the floor. The quick growth stops when the tree has reached the height of the people around it, at which point the room falls into silence.

The silence is then broken by a single metallic songbird that chirps as it comes through a window on the opposite side of the room and circles over the heads of the court. All the heads, including the emperor's, follow its revolutions. Then it settles on a branch of the tree, where it sings an intricate song. All heads turn to the window, from where a song can be heard in reply. And then the film ends.

The smooth growth of the metallic tree, particularly the unfurling of the leaves, proved challenging. Cesarine was able to reuse a bird armature from a previous animation for that part, carefully removing the realistic feathers from the foam form that had been molded around the metal skeleton, painting them with a variety of metallic paints and then replacing them. Although she was not overly concerned with being accurate to Byzantine fashions of the time, she didn't want to be too far off either, so she ended up sneaking into the university's social-science library to do some research, paranoid that her photo had been handed out to the security and library staff and expecting to be apprehended at any moment. In the end, it wasn't just the bird, but all the ideas that were borrowed, so she could play a mechanical role throughout the process, simply assembling the pieces following someone else's plan.

She takes the ideas for the second animation from her hallucinatory experiences with the mechanical woman. The scene is more complex; two realistic blocks, one with houses set back from the street with yards and trees in front, the other lined by two- to three-story commercial buildings built up to a wide sidewalk filled with boulevard trees and street furniture. There are a dozen fully fleshed-out people and a dog that interact in the set. Following her usual style, everything has hatches or viewing ports built in. She used similar blocks in the past, but, since that was before the defection, she has to construct new sets.

Unlike in past films, where everything essentially did what it was supposed to do, nothing in this new world fits quite right. The protagonist, insofar as there is such a creature in her films, is an adolescent girl. She has a hatch under her right ear, but it does not close properly. She leaves her house on the residential block and walks to a store on the commercial side, regularly reclosing the hatch with a movement that resembles an uncontrollable tic. It is a windy day, shown by sporadic movements of the leaves and grass. The panes of the viewing ports in the objects around her are not transparent, but rather are scratched or fogged. The audience can see a vague, shadowy movement behind them, but nothing more. The girl stops to try to clean several panes with her sleeve, but quickly realizes that she isn't accomplishing anything and gives up. She passes a man, whose eye hatch is crudely taped shut with transparent scotch tape. Despite its transparency, a hole is poked through the tape in front of his eye. Hatches in objects are missing knobs or hinge pins, or simply don't fit in their frames, like doors in a house that has shifted.

A maintenance van is parked midway down the residential street. After the girl passes, we hear the breaking of glass. She looks back to see the pane in a tree broken and the maintenance men trying to remove the gears that they find inside. After some effort, it becomes evident that most of the gears are too big for the portal. One of them goes back to the van to get a saw, which they use to make the hole bigger. Once it is large enough, they empty the tree of its inner workings. One of the men notices the girl watching them; he smiles at her before continuing to load the van.

The girl is noticeably troubled by what she is seeing. She does not want to get involved, however, so, after reclosing her hatch with a nervous gesture, she continues on her way to the commercial area. The camera sees one of the men approach her from behind, and then everything goes black. The scene comes back an instant later, with the girl lying on the ground. The truck and the maintenance men are gone; the only sign of their passage is the empty tree that sounds a melancholy note when a gust of wind blows. The girl gets up, checks what she can see and then, not finding anything wrong, heads to her original destination.

The camera can already see the enlarged hole in her head, but she only notices with the next instance of her tic, when she is in the commercial street. She stops dead in her tracks when her hand finds nothing where the hatch used to be. She feels light-headed, both literally and figuratively, and turns to the display window to see her reflection. The display is filled with books; some open, some closed, all with jumbled text that slowly floats within the confines of the covers and pages. This background makes the girl seem unstable, almost illusory, despite her steady, if increasingly agitated, attempts to see what happened to her hatch.

The wind gusts, we can hear the mournful sound of the tree in the distance. We can also hear the girl's head resonate and see the realization of what has happened through the changing expressions of the girl's face in the reflection and through the weakening of her movements. Her final expression is a sadness in harmony with the tree, as she just stares at herself, shoulders slumped. Her arm suddenly jerks up to close her hatch; she forces it back down with her other hand.

Then she is overwhelmed with the sensation of still being conscious, standing, being able to see and hear everything around her. She tests her abilities, misting the window with her breath and writing a sentence and solving some basic equations with her finger. Besides the annoying sound of her head resonating when the wind blows, nothing seems to have changed. She shrugs and starts walking once more. We see crudely enlarged holes in everything in the street as she goes past. Once she has passed them, they join the windblown arpeggio, which becomes increasingly complex and varied, not only in notes but in sentiment. At one point, we see a hatch covered in scotch tape and with a still blinking eye lying on the sidewalk.

The gusts are getting stronger, the arpeggiated notes sound closer together and with more force. When the gusts become a gale, the hollowed-out world gradually disintegrates. The girl has made enough progress for the end of the commercial street to be visible and we can see the van parked in front of the last building. The wind is going in the opposite direction, though, and the girl, leaning forward heavily, is making less and less headway.

She decides to take refuge in the closest building, which has a café on the first floor. The menu offers the standard drink options; oils for those with gears and aggregates, lacquers for those with instruments. She picks an inexpensive oil, just so she can stay. She finds a table in a corner as far from the windows as possible and, without thinking, takes a sip. Moments later, a small trickle of oil escapes from the hole in her head and is absorbed by her shirt. She then looks out at the grey haze that has invaded the street. Occasionally, dark shapes hit the window with the sound of soft flesh against the hard pane.

She almost takes another sip, but stops herself in time. Instead, she goes into the bathroom to clean the stain on her shirt. She looks at her disheveled head in the mirror and tries, once more, to see inside her skull. When that doesn't work, she cleans the shoulder of her shirt the best she can. She pulls a paper towel from the dispenser to dry the spot; as her hand approaches the area, though, she stuffs it into her head. She pauses for a moment and then, with increasingly frantic movements, pulls out more sheets and stuffs them. She hears a deafening ripping sound through the door, followed by wind whistling through the cracks between the door and its frame. None of this registers in the midst of her frenzy.

Suddenly, the noise from beyond the door is silenced. The only sound is the dispenser mechanism being pressed over and over again. The girl takes a while to notice that it is empty. When she does, she turns to look for other objects to fill the emptiness. She starts on the toilet paper, taking whole rolls at a time. There is enough room for the first roll, but, no matter how hard she pushes, the second will not go fully in. She unspools it to wrap enough of the paper around her head to hold it in place. She then looks in the mirror again and laughs spasmodically.

She finally decides to leave the bathroom, to face whatever the world has become. She takes a deep breath and then opens the door. As soon as the door has left its frame, the room collapses, as if that was the only thing holding up the walls. The door stays upright, the handle in her hand, until she notices the futility of it and lets it drop. She looks around her with wide eyes, clearly recognizing nothing.

Multiple vans are parked in random places and an army of workers are busy at a variety of tasks around her. Several are cleaning up the little debris that the wind left behind. Others are constructing a variety of mechanisms in the vague shape of trees, buildings and all the rest. Some are carrying parts and tools from the vans to the sites of the new mechanisms. Where mechanisms have been completed, one is being wrapped with a tree veneer, another with the exterior of a dog. The camera focuses on the head of the girl as the hastily wrapped toilet paper comes apart and both rolls fall to the ground. Her face is a picture of resignation as she collapses in turn. The cleaning crew waits politely to the side until her eyes are closed. Then, they sweep up the bathroom rubble, her shell included.

Cesarine filmed a final scene; a replay of the girl lying on the ground, waking up. When she reaches up to reclose her hatch, she is surprised to find that it is still closed. She continues on her way to the commercial area, only now the view ports are completely clear, showing the minutia of the inner workings in all their glory. In the end, Cesarine decided to not include it in the final cut.

On the whole, Cesarine enjoyed making this one. She didn't focus on technical innovation, but rather on painstaking detail. The facial expressions and body movements of the girl needed to be particularly subtle and almost everything in the set needed to be constantly affected by the wind. It was essentially a refinement of a variety of methods used in her earlier work.

Chapter 21

"Welcome back!" Coralie exclaims, giving Cesarine a hug that the latter isn't entirely comfortable with. "Lucien is still at the center, pretending to work and stealing food."

"Nothing has changed, then? Thank you for putting me up while I am here," Cesarine politely says, trying to add more enthusiasm to her voice than she feels so as to avoid dampening Coralie's mood.

"Our pleasure, any time! I'll show you to your room. For changes, hum, well, Lucien is his usual stick in the mud. My new play, on the other hand, is a great success. *Scapin*, an adaption of one of Molière's works, if you are familiar with that sort of thing. We have a ticket for you for tonight, if you are interested. But first, settle in, make yourself at home."

Cesarine accepts the invitation and follows Coralie to the guestroom. Once she has passed the salon, she notices signs of wear; patched-up furniture and knick-knacks, threadbare rugs, etc.; that could be a stylistic choice but are more likely an indication of hidden poverty. It is not as if Lucien and Coralie put much effort into hiding that they struggle sometimes to get by, but they don't like it to be too blatant, either. Once her luggage is dealt with, the two return to the salon to chat about nothing in particular. She brought a traditional brandy from her old country, so they each have a glass. Coralie says that she will definitely have another, but only after her performance.

Soon after Lucien arrives, with Raoul in tow, Coralie leaves for the theatre. The three follow a while later, after stopping at a restaurant for a bite to eat. Cesarine is mesmerized by the cleverness of the title character of the play, who manages to manipulate everyone with ease for what turns out to be a fairly noble cause. It would be wonderful to have her own Scapin to help her outmaneuver Violet, though that would probably require her plight to be as universally accessible as that of the young lovers he helps in the play. Beyond that, it probably wouldn't hurt for her to be as photogenic as the lovers in question and for her cause to actually be noble. Then again, a team of people far less arrogant than Scapin willing to help her is good too, and would likely prove to be less irritating in the long run.

The next day, her former colleagues arrive and set themselves up in the salon in a way that transforms the space from its usual relaxed atmosphere to a formal meeting room.

"It has been quite some time," Valery says. "I heard about the situation at the university and apologize for that. I also hear that you have made a couple of new films, which is great news. We will, of course, be at the screening tonight."

"Is the conference going well?" Cesarine asks.

"Yes, well enough. Although only time will tell, it looks like the pessimists, those who thought that this was going to be another Yalta are going to be proven wrong. The Russians are not going to walk away with a permanent, internationally recognized border between the two Germanys, while conceding nothing."

"A decision has also been made on 'freedom from fear'," Etienne adds. "It is not going to be in the body of the final document, but in the preamble. The argument that won out was that all the substantive articles already in place would do the work of reducing – even eliminating, one might hope – fear, but that it was important to include it in the beginning as one of the overarching goals of the document. So, you should be proud; not many people can point to a goal that they introduced and to which all the governments of a continent are going to commit."

"I am sure that you three did the vast majority of the work," Cesarine says.

"True, but that does not lessen the importance of you coming up with it in the first place," Rose argues. "In any case, we have another topic on today's agenda."

"Yes, of course," Valery says. "Etienne passed us the note you sent about the possibility of smuggling your work into your old country. You said that you had found a reporter who was willing to do it?"

"Yes, if it was new work," Cesarine replies. "I have, as you mentioned, some new animation, so the question is, can he be trusted or is this another Violet-backed setup?"

"We do not know if Violet is in the picture, although it would not shock me if she was," Rose says. "We have been able to establish that the reporter in question has close ties to the government and makes a suspiciously high number of trips to the embassy. He is definitely not an agent, who would be better about avoiding the embassy, but it is obvious that he can't be trusted."

"That is what I have, too," Etienne adds. "None of my contacts have him as an operative. The state media is run out of the embassy, so it makes sense for him to go there regularly. He is there far too often, though. Given his after-work habits, I would say that he has money problems that his alcoholism is not doing him any favors in dealing with. He is likely just trying to get more money out of his superiors with whatever information he can get his hands on. I imagine that he would get a pretty penny if he showed up with your new films and a story about how you asked him to smuggle the tapes into the country.

"For my money, though, I would bet that Violet is monitoring him as a matter of course, but that she has nothing to do with him in any direct way."

"Lucien talked to him months ago about this. Wouldn't he have gone directly to the embassy with it?" Cesarine asks.

"Maybe," Rose responds, "but, if he did, they would have more than likely laughed in his face. You haven't produced new work in years; without proof, it would have sounded like a desperate ploy."

"Am I still good with the screening tonight?"

"The manager of the cinema is a pillar of the community," Etienne says, "and, in any case, the moment you left the delegation, you stopped being a target for local shenanigans."

"So, now that we all know what we need to know about the original options, what are the other possibilities?" Valery asks.

"We can't use the services of our country," Rose says. "Now that it looks likely that the conference is going to be a success, the direction to avoid any and all provocation has spread everywhere. It is far worse than at the beginning of the conference, and the higher-ups were skittish even then. The detente *über alles*."

"There is no way that we can get the films in through European diplomatic channels, official or not," Etienne says. "If Cesarine was Russian, or even Polish, we would get support, but nobody is willing to use any resources or take any risks with what everyone considers to be an irrelevant country. It is similar to what Rose found; Cesarine's old country has proven itself to be Russia's puppet all through the process, so there is a feeling that such a narrowly targeted effort would have no political effect."

"Which leaves us with Africa," Rose concludes. "Assuming, of course, that Valery still has the right connections."

"We haven't been gone for that long," Valery says. "I was hoping for something more direct, but we know people who can get the films into the country. The difficulty is to find a reliable local contact. That is the advantage of working with the services; they already have assets in place. Ideas?"

"Why don't we send the tapes to Chaulieu?" Etienne asks. "He is, after all, the one who complained that Cesarine's work wasn't available in a convenient format."

"If he is already on Violet's radar," Rose objects, "then he is probably already being watched. Besides, he is a writer, so might not be connected to the people with the equipment to do something with them. What do you think, Cesarine?"

"You're right; as much as I would like to have the tapes sent directly to Chaulieu, it is probably not the best idea. How would they be smuggled in?"

"In a freight shipment from Libya," Valery responds. "I don't know what exactly is being transported."

"If they could be included in a package of materials appropriate for the National School of Puppetry, that would be ideal. It would have to be to the attention of Tonda Keller. Puppeteers have never been politically active, so the government shouldn't be paying much attention to them. Tonda was a student when I was there, and has become a professor since. He appreciated my work back then, but there shouldn't be any records linking us. His own work has been staunchly traditionalist; we didn't have many classes together and, well, I was always in my workshop when I wasn't in class."

"It doesn't sound like he is in a good position to distribute copies of the tapes, assuming that he has kept to the world of puppetry," Etienne says. "That sounds weird when I say it."

"That's the trade-off. Either we send them to someone who is well-connected and watched and risk them being intercepted or to someone unwatched and less connected, and hope that they do something period, first of all, and then that whatever they do actually works. Of course, we can do both; I do have several copies of the films in both formats. I still think that Chaulieu is too high a risk, but if we can come up with other names and Valery's people are willing to send tapes to multiple destinations..."

At that moment, the door to the main bedroom opens and, a second later, Lucien appears at the edge of the salon in a wrinkled t-shirt and shorts. All eyes turn to him.

"Oh, hello, sorry to disturb you, I'll just be a minute."

He goes into the kitchen, where noises of the morning coffee-making ritual can be heard. His head then pops out.

"Would anyone like coffee, or anything else?"

"No, thank you," Rose replies for the group. "We are just about done here."

"Let's just start with Tonda and see how things go," Valery says. "I don't think that it will be too difficult to have the tapes packed in among items appropriate for the school. It is an institution, after all, so all sorts of things, from food and stationary to specialized marionette parts and theatre equipment, must be delivered there all the time. If you give me the tapes, we can have them sent to the appropriate embassy and they can be delivered, with some quick instructions, to the person in question from there. Then it will be out of our hands."

"I could drop them off," Cesarine suggests.

"You want to go to North Africa?"

"Not as such, no, but I don't have anything better to do."

"Okay. Have I ever told you about my friend Robert?"

"Yes, once."

Valery explains how to find Robert's house in the old medina. He suggests that she go to the embassy first and ask for Jack, his former security detail who ended up staying on there after he had left. Jack had been to Robert's place before, which would be useful since an explanation does not really do the tortuous roads and lack of signage in the neighborhood justice.

Once Cesarine has a good idea of where she will be going, the three diplomats rise to leave. Cesarine sees them out. On the doorstep, Etienne repeats that they will all be at the cinema for the screening. He wishes her good luck, in case they don't have a chance to talk before the event. When she returns to the salon, Lucien is sitting on one of the couches, with a French press full of coffee and a tea for her on the coffee table.

"I assumed that the 'no' to a caffeinated beverage did not include you."

"You assumed right."

"Everything went well? You are on the way to becoming the

most notorious animation smuggler of our age?"

"Infamous is my goal."

"I can respect that."

"Your reporter has turned out to be a man who can't be trusted."

"A reporter; I wouldn't trust the whole lot. Especially if they drink, which is a sure sign of the absence of moral fiber."

"Suddenly, everything that I've experienced in your den of iniquity makes sense."

"It's still a mystery to me. I mean, the lack of orgies alone should make one ponder..."

Chapter 22

The manager of the cinema accepted to host another screening despite the fact that the two new films were not long enough to fill an evening. He added several older works that were not shown during the last event and limited the projection to one screen to compensate. Cesarine was just as happy to have a pared-down event, as it would hopefully attract less unwanted attention. Negative reviews of older established works were very different than ones about animation that people were seeing for the first time.

Nobody in the lobby approaches her and she is not inclined to go around initiating conversations and playing host, so Cesarine decides to find a place in the auditorium. She is tempted to choose a seat in the middle, so that she can feel – perhaps even be carried away by – the reactions of the people around her. Since her animation is out in the world, it is part of that world; the point that so many students in her esthetics class had a hard time grasping. Although she is quite fond of what she has done and, when need be, can talk about at least the technical aspects of it endlessly, she has no special, intimate relation with the final object. She has to experience it like everyone else, even if that experience is colored by personal bias.

Besides the practical difficulties of sitting in the middle of a row – she has to make her way to the front for a question and answer session after the screening – she is worried that she will be an emotional sink that dampens the experience of those around her. When she watches her own work as a finished product, she doesn't fully experience it. She loses herself in her own thoughts; in future projects or unrelated ideas. She is sufficiently accustomed to how people who are fully engaged react to her films, so she could always fake it. She could even take a page from the hallucinatory mechanical woman and give an exaggerated reaction that augments the sensations of those around her. The amount of effort required to fake ordinary reaction leaves her cold, though, so she finds a seat at the back where she can appreciate the reactions of the audience without having an influence on them.

Once the audience has settled in, the manager briefly introduces the program. The auditorium is full, so his words are buoyed by the enthusiasm of what is, by all appearances, going to be a successful event. He then joins Cesarine at the back, pulling out a folding chair from an obscure alcove and setting it in the aisle.

"Everything seems to be coming together nicely," he says to Cesarine. "Thank you again for coming back into town for one of these. I'm really excited to see your new shorts."

"Thank you for the invitation," Cesarine replies politely.

As the lights dim, Cesarine feels a shock of fear; no doubt an aftershock from the previous projection in the space. She feverishly scans the crowd for Violet, convinced that she must be there somewhere. She nervously waits for the waves of contradictory emotions to roll through the crowd, reshaping the reactions to what is on the screen. Then panic hits her as her mind tries to conjure up the waves of sentiments pulling, draining the energy from the crowd and, instead, gives her the sensation of stepping off a cliff into nothingness. She closes her eyes as the world continues on normally and searches desperately for whatever is left of her functional indifference.

When she reopens her eyes, she notices that the manager is looking at her with a worried expression. He leans forward, about to say something, when he is interrupted by an employee who needs his attention elsewhere in the theatre. He squeezes Cesarine's hand, smiles reassuringly and then disappears, leaving the empty chair behind him.

Cesarine stares at the chair, her mind convulsing. Everything of substance in her leads her to be convinced that this empty chair is an open invitation for Violet to join her, then that she has; that she is there, right beside her, somehow managing to be engrossed in the film and analyze her at the same time. All that she can see, all that she can imagine, is the empty space. She hesitatingly reaches out with her hand, only to find the emptiness confirmed. Yet, she is absolutely sure that someone is there.

Suddenly, someone is there; a dark shape that she can't quite make out. She stifles a scream, suppresses her urge to run, closes her eyes, takes a breath and forces herself to think of indifference. In her mind, she finds herself walking along the streets to the school, her emotions diminished with every step. She can't make out the streets, but knows somehow that that is where she is. Her compulsion to imagine them fades to apathy. She reopens her eyes to find that it is just Lucien beside her, looking at her with quizzical amusement.

"If I didn't know better," he whispers, "I would say that you had a vision of your dear evil sister. Do you want to step out into the lobby?"

Cesarine shakes her head, already much calmer. The panic makes way for a cold anger at herself for being overwhelmed by such an absurd fear, particularly after so much time has passed. She made it through the screening right after the original theatre nightmare with aplomb, so to not be able to control herself now seems to her to be utterly ridiculous.

Lucien shrugs and shifts his attention to the screen.

The rest of the projection goes smoothly. It turns out that, if one cannot imagine the street part of walking down a street that holds certain well-established emotional connotations, the emotional connotations are all that is left. In this instance, it is like moving through a cloud of distilled apathy. Once Cesarine has had enough of being angry at herself – spilled milk and all that – she loses herself in this cloud. She can still make out the regular, predictable reactions of the audience to what they are watching, can still sense how the sensations are amplified and reinforced by the group experience, but can't bring herself to be a part of it.

When the screening is over, she goes up to the front and gives technical answers to all the questions posed, technical or not. Then she goes to the lobby for the reception. She is quickly joined by Coralie and her chorus, who expertly deflect the more annoying and inappropriate questions and requests. It is clear that Lucien said something to them about her panic attack.

"That turned out well," Lucien says after Cesarine's popularity has died down.

"When you weren't here at the beginning, we thought you have been kidnapped," Henry says to Lucien. "Missing an opportunity to see your sorceress's magic seemed unthinkable."

"I wagered that you had been run over by a train," Jack points out.

"Killed in a duel," Raoul adds.

"Arrested for something shameful, then you hanged yourself in your cell," Eugene concludes.

"That's not morbid at all," Coralie says.

"To be honest," Lucien sighs, "I was delayed by the unthinkable; an article, if you can believe it. I got a last-minute call from a British publication wanting a piece on how ratification of the final conference document was supposed to work for federated states. They must have been desperate to call me, though it's hard to imagine that a subject like that could lead to desperation. Apparently, it came out of recent talk of devolving power to a Scottish assembly.

"Anyway, I was able to take Clive's chair and I arrived in time for the two new films. I have to say that I was not expecting the mechanical tree. It was brilliant, and a sign that you should listen to me more often. Just imagine what you could do with... Ah, hello again."

Lucien switches gears as Valery, Rose and Etienne appear. The three stop by briefly to congratulate Cesarine and wish her luck with her future endeavors. When they are gone, Lucien's train of thought has passed by and the conversation continues without it.

"If there was any question about the real impact of our reviews, I think it has been settled tonight," Jack says. "Granted that it was only one screen this time around, but the turnout was still excellent."

"Are you going to write some better reviews this time around?" Coralie asks.

"There isn't much point with a one-evening event," Raoul replies. "If it had a run of even a week, there would be more incentive."

"Without a generous, albeit malevolent, backer, the usual game must be played," Jack explains. "Not only will readers not be interested in reading a review for something they can't go see, there won't be any tickets to sell. No tickets makes for sad, sober hack reporters; nobody wants that."

"We can ask around though, see if any editors are interested," Henry says. "Are there showings planned for other cities? Are they going to be available in other formats?"

"There are no plans for them at the moment," Cesarine says. "I am working on a distribution deal for them in other formats, but I don't know how successful that's going to be. Even if the deal works out, though, it would not be in a market you guys write for."

"Sounds like the perfect opportunity to be honest," Coralie suggests. "You don't have to worry about buzz or controversy, let alone keeping to an editorial line set by an anonymous backer. You can view this as an experiment to see if your usual outlets would even consider such a thing."

"You are assuming that we have our own opinion," Raoul says. "I don't think any of us has a single opinion about much of anything anymore."

"Well, maybe Lucien does," Jack adds, "but, given the circumstances, he won't be much use, either. Still, as Henry said, we'll see."

"And, as Henry says now; I hear that Cesarine brought brandy from her old country, brandy that is at this very moment sad and alone at Coralie's place. I suggest that we join it."

"I am going to go find Clive to make sure that there is nothing else to be done," Cesarine says, searching the rapidly thinning crowd for the manager. "Then, we can go."

She motions to the manager as he comes out of the second auditorium.

"I'm sorry I had to leave when I did," Clive says. "You didn't seem well."

"You passed Lucien in the lobby, I assume."

"Yes. I mentioned my concern, I hope you don't mind."

"It is perfectly fine; there is no reason to apologize."

"Good, good. So, obviously, that was a great success. Thank you very much coming. We don't get many filmmakers willing to do Q and As here; the market isn't big enough, I suppose. This is a good testing ground, though; with so many foreigners living here, there is a great deal of diversity.

"Speaking of diversity, I heard a lot of appreciation for *The Mechanical Tree*. While it stayed with the overall mechanical theme, it was quite different than your usual work. The audience found it refreshing. Take that how you will, of course.

"Other than that, if you have more new work, drop me a line. Next time, we might even be able to arrange a bit of a tour. If I ever get out of here, I might see you at Coralie's later, but don't hold your breath."

They shake hands and he is immediately off to put out the next fire of the evening.

Cesarine rejoins her chorus and they head to Coralie and Lucien's place. She would prefer to be alone so she can drop the mask she has barely been able to keep on all evening. The only time that she was comfortable was when she was going on about the technical challenges of her films. Everything else was misdirection. She promises herself to retreat to her bedroom after one brandy.

Chapter 23

Robert is sitting with Cesarine and Jack from the embassy at the small round table in the inner courtyard of his house. He prepares mint tea while the other two look on in silence. Everyone is relaxed, a world away from anything happening beyond the walls. A knock on the door rings out, which puts a frown on Robert's face. He takes another cup from the tray and, when the tea is ready, fills four cups. Then he rises slowly and goes to the door.

A joyful "Valery, it has been too long!", completely at odds with Robert's countenance before he opened the door, can be heard clearly by Jack and Cesarine. An instant later, the two men enter the courtyard, speaking to each other in hushed tones, and join the others at the table.

"It looks like my timing is perfect," Valery says, looking at the tea.

"Not quite," Robert responds. "I was in the middle of making it when you knocked."

"Luckily, you are not easily distracted."

"Yes, quite. What brings you here, Valery? You can't have any bad tidings; those duties have been relegated to young Jack, here. He has become something of an expert in informing me in a tasteful manner that one of my relatives has passed. I get the impression that he is aiming to graduate from tasteful to delicate, no matter how many times I remind him that, if he went there, I would probably not cotton on to the fact that the relation in question was well and truly dead."

"I would chalk it up to the exuberance of youth. It will likely pass."

Jack is unable to keep a straight face and starts laughing, before putting an end to it with a sip of tea and mumbling a vague apology.

"How did you end up with obituary duty?" Valery asks Jack.

"After you and Rose left, it turns out that I was the only one who knew how to get here. I was twiddling my thumbs most of the time, so I volunteered. At first, it was just to make myself useful, but I have to say that Robert's tea, if not the man himself, has really grown on me."

"And you, Cesarine, you decided to stay?"

"Robert was gracious enough to have me."

"She hasn't been too much trouble?" Valery asks Robert.

"She is so busy with her toys, one would hardly know she was around most of the time. Some of the rooms that haven't been touched since the family fled are being used again, which is a good thing. It was time to move on."

Valery turns to Cesarine. "Does this mean that you are starting to create again?"

"No. I am just trying out some different ideas."

"Fair enough. Although, I have to say that I would love to see more of your work. I especially liked *The Mechanical Tree*."

"She also set up a screening room," Robert continues. "We now have movie nights, which, it is safe to say, is a shock to us all. What did we see last week? Oh, yes; *Closely Watched Trains*. That movie has a great deal of merit."

"You like it here, then?" Valery asks Cesarine.

"Marshall M___ undoubtedly liked the old medina, even if no one in Africa seemed to like him."

"Can you blame them?" Robert asks rhetorically. "What an incompetent twit."

"That was a bit of a non-sequitur," Valery says. "First, Robert; one could argue that he was, on the whole, a very competent twit. He did, after all, reach the height of power later in his career. It is somewhat unfair to judge someone solely on the lowest point of their professional life. Meddling in North Africa marked the nadir of the careers of many very accomplished figures.

"Second, Cesarine; what does Marshall M___ have to do with anything?"

"He said that the city I was living in before was not conducive of public effervescence, largely because of its perfectly engineered and utterly characterless streets. Having passed along those streets countless times in the years I was there, I think it is clear that he was right – despite whatever other failings of character he may have had. The streets here are the complete opposite, and I find it very pleasant. Though, before you ask; no, that does not help me be a better artist or anything else."

"You don't mind how touristic it has become?"

"I don't have a point of reference for how it was before. Though, from what I understand, it is just as well that I am here now. I am not, as it happens, very observant, so I would have probably walked into unfortunate situations without knowing it. I prefer my fear to come from snow puddles, and not rampant crime."

Robert nods. "For her, it is definitely better now."

"Should I ask about the snow puddles?" Valery asks.

"Best not," Jack responds. "She'll just give you the book and say that she will be happy to discuss it with you when you've finished it. I haven't finished it, though, so you'll have to stay in the dark for now."

"Ah. I will leave it be, then."

"We did have to replace all the wiring in the place, so that all the fancy equipment could run without overloading everything and causing a fire," Robert says.

"Okay, good to know."

"You still haven't told us the purpose for your visit."

"Right, sorry. I got caught up in all the news. I'm mainly here to see Cesarine, to talk to her about something that came out of the conference."

Valery leans over, searches in his bag and then pulls out an issue of their country's left-leaning national newspaper. He then unfolds it and hands it to Cesarine. While Cesarine reads the first several pages, Valery explains to the others what she is looking at.

"It is a charter written by dissidents of Cesarine's old country and signed by an impressive range of citizens. It goes over the obligations that the government has set for itself, both through the constitution and international agreements to which it is a signatory, and details its shortcomings. It demands that the government live up to its responsibilities. One of the most-cited agreements, particularly in regards to human rights, is the covenant that came out of the conference Cesarine was a part of.

"It is too early to tell what the full impact will be. All we know is that there have been several arrests and that the government is working on a counter-charter of its own. The world has not become a wonderful place overnight. That said, the covenant is already being used by civil groups in a variety of countries as a justification to demand more from their government. I, as is usually the case, choose to be hopeful; we have managed to provide a tool for people who are looking to effect change. Despite all the rest, you should be proud of playing a role in creating it."

"Did 'freedom from fear' make it into the charter?" Cesarine asks without looking up.

"No. It was never an article, so does not have the same weight as other parts of the text. It would be used more for interpreting the intent of clauses. On the other hand, the right of residency is included."

"This means that the conference is over, no?" Robert asks.

"Yes. It took a lot longer than anybody anticipated. The Russians threatened to walk away at least a half-dozen times because it was taking so long. But, finally, we came to an agreement."

"Are you coming back?"

"No. Funnily enough, there is a series of follow-up conferences to make sure that the implementation of the covenant stays on track. Contrary to what many people predicted, the covenant is not going to gather dust on a shelf. This is to say that we are already preparing for the next round, in addition to putting a standing committee together and fulfilling a pile of other requirements set out in the document. I will probably be in town from time to time, since I was involved in so many projects here over the years, but it is looking like I will be in Europe until my retirement."

"What about the border between the Germanys?" Cesarine asks.

"The document includes it – it had to, given the intentions of Russia and East Germany – but it is not binding. That is actually the main reason why the final text ended up taking the form of a covenant and not a treaty; if it was a treaty, all the signatories would be bound to respect the line. That is not the case with a covenant."

"But then, nobody is bound to respect anything else," Jack points out.

"True, but that doesn't matter. The international community was never going to take a hard line on enforcing rights of expression and all the rest. The whole effort was intended as a nudge in what we would like to think is the right direction. It is cover, not only for civil groups, but also for countries like Poland to differentiate themselves from the Soviet Union. It is a document countries can point to during bilateral meetings. It is very soft power, but that does not make it ineffective."

"Tonda Keller signed it," Cesarine says, looking up. "That reminds me; sending the tapes to him had some bizarre repercussions. It kind of opened the floodgates in the other direction. A couple of weeks after the package was delivered to the school, it was sent back to Robert's distributors with a note saying that the shipment was incomplete. They said that it looked unopened, and we didn't want more people knowing that my tapes were in there, so Robert had it sent back to his local warehouse. When we opened it, we found tapes, but they weren't mine. It was obvious that they were from people at the school, but the work was modern, experimental; not the usual, traditional fare that the censors have never cared about.

"We sat on them for a while, and then I had the idea of sending them to someone I trust at the School of Marionettes. The school ended up distributing them under its own banner, which, as I understand it, was a way of thumbing their nose at the university's excessive risk aversion. Amusingly, the prestige associated with the exclusive distribution was such that university officials apparently claimed after the fact to be on board since the beginning.

"Since then, Robert has been obliging enough to send a package to the School of Puppetry whenever it blends in with his usual operations. They never overdo it – there are never more than a couple of tapes – so we've become comfortable with the arrangement. Arguably, the next step is to include tapes from Marionettes in the packages going in, but we haven't gotten there yet. And really, it's Robert taking all the risk."

Robert shrugs. "I've said it before, but you have a strange notion of risk."

"I've lived a sheltered life."

"That, you have."

"Wow!" Valery exclaims. "This is a huge step for you, and very unexpected. You've always avoided involvement with other groups, especially dissident artist communities, and here you are at the center of a movie-smuggling operation. I'm stunned."

"You are reading too much into it," Cesarine says. "I am not a part of any community, and still don't care much for them. So long as Robert is okay with continuing on this path, it seems like the thing to do. However, we are just the middlemen; we merely fulfill a logistics function. And, of course, we watch what comes through, but that is neither here nor there."

"Some of them are really good," Robert interjects.

"Right, well, downplay it all you like, but cross-cultural exchanges like this make Europe a better place. They remind everyone that the people on the other side of the curtain are human beings, and not ideological monsters."

"I'll keep it in mind." Cesarine goes back to reading the list of names. "It looks like most of the puppeteers I knew signed. That's unusual."

"You haven't had any run-ins with Violet since the conference, I hope?"

"No, thankfully. You?"

"No. Etienne is keeping an eye out, though."

"How are Etienne and Rose?"

"Good, though the team has broken up since the conference finished. Etienne is back with NATO, but might be rejoining me when we get closer to the next conference. Rose is head of mission at a major embassy in the Americas. She was hoping to stay in Europe, but is content so long as she stays out of Africa. She has already made it known that, while she appreciates the opportunity the conference gave her, she would never do it again."

"Look at that; Lora and Léon Chaulieu signed. I guess I shouldn't be surprised, in his case at least. Why wouldn't someone who runs an underground newspaper sign something like this?"

"It would make sense." Valery turns to Robert. "Thank you for the tea. I will be back the next time I am in town, and I expect that, by then, you will be completely transformed into a film snob."

"It is always a pleasure, Valery, and you are always welcome."

"I should probably get back to the embassy, too," Jack says.

The three of them rise. Cesarine hands the newspaper to Valery.

"Keep it," he says. "A memento of sorts."

The three men head to the door, leaving Cesarine alone at the table. She finishes her tea and heads to her workshop, leaving the newspaper behind.

At Roundfire we publish great stories. We lean towards the spiritual and thought-provoking. But whether it's literary or popular, a gentle tale or a pulsating thriller, the connecting theme in all Roundfire fiction titles is that once you pick them up you won't want to put them down.

If you have enjoyed this book, why not tell other readers
by posting a review on your preferred booksite.
Recent bestsellers from Roundfire are:

The Bookseller's Sonnets
Andi Rosenthal
The Bookseller's Sonnets intertwines three love stories with a
tale of religious identity and mystery spanning five hundred
years and three countries.
Paperback: 978-1-84694-342-3 e-book: 978-184694-626-4

Birds of the Nile
An Egyptian Adventure
N.E. David
Ex-diplomat Michael Blake wanted a quiet birding trip up the
Nile – he wasn't expecting a revolution.
Paperback: 978-1-78279-158-4 e-book: 978-1-78279-157-7

Blood Profit$
The Lithium Conspiracy
J. Victor Tomaszek, James N. Patrick, Sr
The blood of the many for the profits of the few… Blood Profit$
will take you into the cigar-smoke-filled room where American
policy and laws are really made.
Paperback: 978-1-78279-483-7 e-book: 978-1-78279-277-2

The Burden
A Family Saga
N.E. David
Frank will do anything to keep his mother and father apart. But
he's carrying baggage – and it might just weigh him down...
Paperback: 978-1-78279-936-8 e-book: 978-1-78279-937-5

The Cause
Roderick Vincent
The second American Revolution will be a fire lit from an internal spark.
Paperback: 978-1-78279-763-0 e-book: 978-1-78279-762-3

Don't Drink and Fly
The Story of Bernice O'Hanlon Part One
Cathie Devitt
Bernice is a witch living in Glasgow. She loses her way in her life and wanders off the beaten track looking for the garden of enlightenment.
Paperback: 978-1-78279-016-7 e-book: 978-1-78279-015-0

Gag
Melissa Unger
One rainy afternoon in a Brooklyn diner, Peter Howland punctures an egg with his fork. Repulsed, Peter pushes the plate away and never eats again.
Paperback: 978-1-78279-564-3 e-book: 978-1-78279-563-6

The Master Yeshua
The Undiscovered Gospel of Joseph
Joyce Luck
Jesus is not who you think he is. The year is 75 CE. Joseph ben Jude is frail and ailing, but he has a prophecy to fulfil…
Paperback: 978-1-78279-974-0 e-book: 978-1-78279-975-7

On the Far Side, There's a Boy
Paula Coston
Martine Haslett, a thirty-something 1980s woman, plays hard on the fringes of the London drag club scene until one night which prompts her to sign up to a charity. She writes to a young Sri Lankan boy, with consequences far and long.

Paperback: 978-1-78279-574-2 e-book: 978-1-78279-573-5

Tuareg
Alberto Vazquez-Figueroa
With over 5 million copies sold worldwide, Tuareg is a classic adventure story from best-selling author Alberto Vazquez-Figueroa, about honour, revenge and a clash of cultures.
Paperback: 978-1-84694-192-4

Find more titles and sign up to our readers' newsletter at http://www.johnhuntpublishing.com/fiction

Follow us on Facebook at https://www.facebook.com/JHPfiction and Twitter at https://twitter.com/JHPFiction

Most titles are published in paperback and as an e-book. Paperbacks are available in physical bookshops. Both print and e-book: editions are available online. Readers of e-books can click on the live links in the titles to order.